Tending the Remnant Damage

To Marilyn -
glad to finally meet you.
Banff, May/2002.
Sheila Peters

Tending the Remnant Damage

stories by

Sheila Peters

Porcepic Books
an imprint of

Beach Holme Publishing
Vancouver

First Edition

This book is published by Beach Holme Publishing, 226-2040 West 12th Avenue, Vancouver, B.C. V6J 2G2 *www.beachholme.bc.ca*. This is a Porcepic Book.

The publisher gratefully acknowledges the financial support of the Canada Council for the Arts and of the British Columbia Arts Council. The publisher also acknowledges the financial assistance received from the Government of Canada through the Book Publishing Industry Development Program (BPIDP) for its publishing activities.

Editor: Michael Carroll
Production and Design: Jen Hamilton
Cover Art: Photograph by Harry Kruisselbrink copyright © 1975.
Used with the permission of the artist.
Author Photograph: Pat Moss

Printed and bound in Canada by Houghton Boston

National Library of Canada Cataloguing in Publication Data

Peters, Sheila, 1953-
Tending the remnant damage

"A Porcepic book."
ISBN 0-88878-417-1

I. Title.
PS8581.E747T46 2001 C813'.6 C2001-910121-X
PR9199.3.P47T46 2001

For Lynn Shervill

Contents

Acknowledgements ix

The Belair Beach Bar Roundup 1
Shooting in the Dark 11
Hecate Strait 25
Divining Isaac 47
Disappearance 61
A Fool's Paradise 83
Tending the Remnant Damage 105
Cultivation 125
Delivery 137
Breathing Fire 149

Acknowledgements

The following stories were previously published: "Disappearance" (*NeWest Review*); "The Belair Beach Bar Roundup" (*creekstones: words & images*); "Cultivation" (*Room of One's Own*); "Delivery" (*Grain*); "Shooting in the Dark" (*Prism international*); and "Tending the Remnant Damage" (*The Malahat Review*).

In "Hecate Strait" several lines of poetry are embedded in the text. The italicized lines in the following text from that story are from Mary Oliver's poem "I Looked Up," published in *White Pine* by Harcourt Brace and used with its permission: "I read poetry when the short heat of summer leaches into September frosts. *What misery to be afraid of death.* In my kitchen overlooking an ancient gully where seasons rise and subside, I tamp mint leaves into a tea ball. The clay cup warms my hand. I am a visitor here in spite of thirty years. *What wretchedness, to believe only in what can be proven.* I am alone."

The following italicized lines in "Hecate Strait" are from Robert Bringhurst's poem "Sutra of the Heart," published in *Pieces of Map, Pieces of Music* by McClelland & Stewart and quoted here with the author's permission:

> *The heart is three bowls full and one empty,* I think. *The heart is a full set of goatprints.*
>
> *The heart is a white mountain*
> *left of centre in the world.*

The heart is dust. The heart is trees.
The heart is snowbound broken
rock in the locked ribs of a man
in the sun on the shore of the sea who is dreaming
sun on the snow, dreaming snow on the broken
rock, dreaming wind, dreaming winter.

My voice fades into the autumn twilight.
What else? he asks.
I thought he was asleep. It's hard to remember, I say.
He turns to look at me, waiting.

The heart is four hands serving soup
made of live meat and water.
The heart is a place. The heart is a name.

The final italicized lines in "Hecate Strait" are from Jan Zwicky's poem "You Must Believe in Spring" in *Songs for Relinquishing the Earth,* published by Brick Books and quoted here with the author's permission: "*Because even sorrow has a source,* I say. *For, though it cannot fly, the heart is an excellent clamberer.*"

The author thanks the Canada Council and her colleagues at Northwest Community College for the time and space to complete this project; Harry Kruisselbrink for his patience and perspective; Will Lawson for his attentive eye and spirit; Jeanie Elsner and Alan Pickard for their early readings of many of the stories; Gail's Green Grocery for just the right food at just the right time, every time; Myrna, Doretta, and Jake for their generous hearts; Ross Hoffman for bringing a little prairie smoke to the mountains; David and Janet Walford at Mountain Eagle Books for proving everything is possible; Dr. Thomas Power, a Montana economist, for coming to Smithers and saying something like this: "A big company will promise a small town everything. Then when it's taken the resources it came for, it pulls up stakes and leaves the community tending the remnant damage"; and to Richard Jenne for noticing.

Which is not to say
there is no joy—only that
it's never a reward...
the sweetest truth, or the most terrible,
can fly up, just like that, be lost
like dust in sunlight.

—Jan Zwicky, "Beethoven: Op. 95"

The Belair Beach Bar Roundup

Chloe inhales the salt-washed Queen Charlotte Islands air and pretends it's cigarette smoke flowing into her lungs, sending treacherous fingers out into the bronchial trees, slipping into all the tiny pleural sacs to sow seeds for the flowering of tumours. Exhaling, she watches the girl whose house she is staying in walk toward her with an armload of tangled fish net. When the girl sees Chloe, she stops, as Chloe knew she would, and turns away. She drifts toward a cedar snag, hooks one end of the net onto the stub of a branch, and starts to untangle it.

Chloe's hair was long when she came to plant trees on the islands that spring. The incessant wind tangled stray wisps no matter how she braided or tied it. She'd hacked it short in the middle of a windy beach party. The next morning Wy, her boyfriend, shaved her head in the girl's kitchen.

Chloe had her eyes closed, savouring the coolness of air on her scalp, when the girl screamed. Wy thought it was the mess of hair, but when she looked at her strange new self in the mirror, Chloe understood. Baldness. Cancer. The girl's parents had left her alone in their big house on the beach while one of them slowly died in Vancouver. It isn't clear which. After each evening's phone call, the girl goes to her room and shuts the door.

Since the party, Chloe's hair has grown into blond fuzz, but the girl still won't come near. Chloe finds this a relief. She can't bear watching the girl crawl off the couch to begin another futile chore after watching television for hours. Emptying cupboards to scrub them, then leaving the dishes scattered on the floor. Or like now. Draping tattered fish net between trees, as if she might mend it, or plant morning glories to climb it. In late August.

Chloe wishes a customer would come. The Belair Beach Bar, a blue tarp stretched over a frame of two-by-fours, stands in one of the few patches of sunlight on the tree-shrouded road between the Masset air force base and Tow Hill. A long extension cord connects its fridge full of Coke, iced tea, and chocolate bars to the girl's house shuttered behind the cedars. Stacks of potato- and corn-chip boxes form one wall. Cases of bootleg beer for the neighbours are hidden in a cooler under thick salal. Two round plastic tables and a few chairs tilt drunkenly in the sand.

On Saturdays Wy barbecues hot dogs, hamburgers, chicken, and salmon. Then it's a party. Now it's tedium. Chloe is a radiology student between her first and second years. She's watched many tumours bloom, wondering why people smoked. Now she understands. Something, anything, to break the monotony.

The Beach Bar is Wy's invention. Wy, short for Wyatt. His mom loved Wyatt Earp. He used to hate his name but now uses it to get people talking. People tell him everything. That's how they got to stay in the girl's house. He was the only one she'd talk to the day they found her crying on the beach.

The girl has picked up a rock and is trying to pound twigs into the ground to stake down the net. Chloe watches the clumsy rock, the girl's awkward fingers, the rotten twigs shredding beneath the blows. Chloe isn't heartless. She'd like to help and thinks the girl's parents are awful. She imagines telling them this and comforting the girl, who reminds her of the teenagers in the psych ward where she visited a friend. All those girls who cut themselves.

Chloe shivers. There's no warmth left in the damp air trapped beneath the lattice of cedar and hemlock. The heat is leaching out with the summer. And with it, her certainty. She'd been the one to talk Wy into coming to the Charlottes. He was ambling through some business courses; she wanted an adventure before she finished school and started work.

"I can't stand the thought of living an unopened life," she'd told Wy. "People know their lives are a wonderful gift. But the packaging distracts them. They spend so many careful years trying to untie the ribbon that they're facing death before they understand what their life should be. I don't want to wait until it's too late."

Wy said Chloe had spent too much time watching the secret, damaged places inside people's bodies. "People get opened up all the time. It's not recommended. And if they wake up at all, they're the same old person with tattered ribbon." He ducked her irritated swat.

"I feel like I'm not experiencing life directly. There's something in between the me that lives in here and the chattering ninny that exits through here." She pinched her lips.

Wy leaned in to whisper. "All that's inside this delectable package is blood, bone, muscle, nerve endings. Enjoy them." His hands moved. "I do."

But he came with her. Planted trees. Watched whales in the wide blue ocean. Loved it all. He found the girl and the house, set up the Beach Bar, hired two Haida kids to help. At first Chloe felt the same. Walking into storm-force winds on North Beach, the surf crashing over her bare feet, had, she thought, washed her clean. Opened her up for life.

But she is hesitant now as she sits, bored, in what passes for the corner store on the tourist trail to Tow Hill and the long arc of North Beach sand.

"Do we stay or go?" Wy had asked that morning. "Do we keep living or go back to school?"

Wy thinks of them as a couple. She's not sure about that either. She closes her eyes and tries to imagine her very own life.

She hears the girl behind her, still untangling the net. The girl's been blown wide open, come right apart. Chloe can imagine the girl's pain and confusion. But not her own life. Not here. Not anywhere. She has lost her momentum. Is that what turns two people into a couple? One loses momentum?

Chloe hears a car. A white Cadillac fishtails into the driveway and ploughs to a stop on the sand in front of her. When Wy jumps out and yells, "Ta da!" the picture doesn't register. She sees his skin, black curly hair, and flashing teeth as if for the first time.

"Earth to Chloe, come in." He waves to the girl, then pulls Chloe to the car. "Look."

She puts her head through the open window and smells the air freshener dangling from the rearview mirror. Red upholstery, electric windows, and locks.

She straightens. "Where's the eight-track?"

"You can't have everything. But what's mine is yours." He tosses her the keys.

"This is yours?" She squints into the sun behind him. She can't see his face properly.

"Partly. I have done the deed. My tuition money has been redirected. I am now a junior partner in Queen Charlotte Automobile Lease and Service Centre."

"What?"

"I've been thinking. I don't want a job, I don't want a profession, I want to do business. Remember that woman from the barbecue last week? We got talking and she needs help. She's a mechanic, but she needs a front man. It's perfect. I might as well get started." He leans in close, and Chloe can feel his breath against her cheek. "I have cut the ribbon on the package."

Chloe's fury is white-hot.

He dances away, whirling in the sand. "Tonight we celebrate. The kids from the village are rounding up saltwater protein. The fiddlers from Tlell have been forewarned. The first annual Belair Beach Bar Roundup will begin at low tide."

"What do you mean, *we* celebrate? Where exactly is the *we* in all this? I don't recall discussing it."

Wy stops. "Whoa. Wait a minute. Wasn't it you who said all that stuff about breaking open?" He reaches for her.

She hits his hand. "Renting cars? Your life maybe. But it has nothing to do with me." She throws the keys on the sand. They lie there between them, glittering in the wind-washed silence.

Chloe is expecting Wy to keep talking. To turn it into a joke, to explain where she fits in here. She is surprised when he turns and walks down the road toward the beach.

"Let's finish this!" she screams as he disappears into the gloom of cedars. When she moves to follow him, fingers hold her shoulder. A hand brushes her head. Spooked by the girl's touch, Chloe freezes. The girl stoops and hands her the keys to the Cadillac.

⁂

Wy is talking to a tourist where the road and the tea-coloured Hiellen River run out onto North Beach. Miles of sand and Alaska invisible in the distance. Chloe waves as she cranks the Cadillac around onto the beach, sending a rooster tail of sand over the men. She laughs at Wy's surprise and ignores his yells as he runs after her, signalling her to stop. Chloe is already shaping the story of her grand exit, making jokes about the shocked and disapproving hikers she will sail past, waving like the queen. Even though this road lasts only as long as the tide allows.

⁂

"There's a hummingbird trapped in my car."

Finn looks up from his plate at Chloe, who is shuffling her bare feet at the door of his tent. Chloe knows him, sort of. Has seen his salt-caked hair and awkward bulk somewhere, at some party maybe. Heard he was counting birds on Rose Spit where North Beach trails into Dixon Entrance. Didn't much like people. Startled hikers. Laughed at trucks stuck in the sand. Stuck like Wy's Cadillac. She looks around the tent, at the books, the table and chair, the comforting sense of a room.

He rises. "A hummingbird?"

She backs out of the tent. "Down here. It flew in as I was contemplating my doom."

He follows.

North Beach sand turns to gravel as it nears the spit. Gravel that sucks in spinning tires. Chloe had revved the engine a few times before accepting that the car was irrevocably stuck. When she turned off the engine and let the sounds of the twittering shorebirds fill the sudden quiet, she was still caught up in the drama of her fury. She was mostly amused, convinced that Wy wasn't serious. Then the hummingbird flew in the window and buzzed against the windshield like an angry wasp. Afraid it would pierce her eyes, she jumped out and opened all the doors, but the bird flung itself repeatedly at the glass.

When she brings Finn to the Cadillac, slumped up to its hubs in gravel, the bird is huddled against the back window. As they approach, it begins again its frantic bashing. He climbs in. His T-shirt strains across the muscles of his back as he stretches toward the bird. He gathers it tenderly in his big hands, slides out, and holds it toward her.

"I'm afraid."

"Hold him firmly so he can't hurt himself." He feeds the bird into her tentative fingers, keeping his own hands around hers so she can't fling it away as she immediately wants to, to get rid of the scrabbling claws.

"He can't hurt you."

He's right. The claws tickle. Chloe barely breathes as she watches the pulse in the bird's ruby throat. She sees her hands enveloped in his, feels the pulse in her own throat.

"Okay. That's enough." He opens his hands, pulling hers open with them. The bird streaks into brightness.

Chloe watches, wistful. "Thank you."

"I'm surprised to see one still here. I watched a pair mating in June but haven't seen them for weeks. The red upholstery must have caught his attention. Don't see many Cadillacs out this far."

He looks down at the tires. "You are definitely stuck. The

tide's on its way out, but it'll be back up this far about midnight. Your car is going to get wet."

"It's not mine. I don't care." She flops in the sand, leans against a log, and puts her feet up on another. He sits beside her feet and picks one up. Holding it firmly, he runs his hand along its edge. "I've seen these somewhere before."

"They've been around all summer." She pulls her foot away. "Haven't carried me very far, though. I feel just as stuck as that bird was. Perfectly free to go wherever I want, but as trapped as a gopher in a snare."

"A gopher in a snare would likely be dead." He picks up her other foot and pulls it against the soft cotton of his faded T-shirt as if to measure the height of the arch. "She's on her way now."

"But she had help."

"So what's wrong with help? Anyway, she would have figured it out eventually. Unlike the gopher. Or the car." Sliding down, he puts the surprised arch of her foot against his lips.

"Hey!" She yanks her foot back and jumps up.

Finn shrugs. "Just checking. I've been tracking birds all summer. Makes me obsess a little on feet." He stands. "And yours have quite a workout ahead. I'll grab my pack and walk back with you."

The walk from Rose Spit to Tow Hill is long. Chloe knows this, having done it once. But she is half expecting Wy to come looking for her or the car. At first she hopes he won't, because she's enjoying the buzz she feels watching Finn move on the sand.

He tells her he has walked the beach so many times, he could do it with his eyes closed and still know when he's nearing Tow Hill. But he keeps his eyes open, counts birds, examines their feed, notes what's washed up. He nudges mounds of kelp and purple jellyfish with his boot, reminding her of the weather and tides from a week ago. They walk at the edge of the water. He sometimes lags behind.

"To see how fast your footprints fill with water," he says.

Chloe has never been as conscious of her feet and calves. She imagines she knows how the birds feel under his gaze. As the miles pass, she feels the spring leave her step. She is hungry.

Daylight fades into the grey sand, the silver water. Chloe feels as if she's walking in folds of shimmering grey silk until, finally, firelight rises and gives shape to the shoreline.

"Incoming party," Finn says.

"The Belair Beach Bar Roundup."

The firelight grows as they approach, grows into a great ring of separate fires. It turns the night air black, the sand dark, the water dark, the only silver a streak where phosphorescent algae glitter in a gentle wash.

When the drums begin, Finn tells her he feels like a solitary sanderling blown in from the High Arctic, shaking his feathers and homing in on a flock of what he hopes are his own. He's been alone so much this summer he's not sure anymore what characteristics identify his species, he says. And steps into the ring of fires.

Chloe stops at the edge, feeling as if a strong wind at her back has dropped her, heavy and becalmed. Are these my friends? she wonders, looking at the familiar faces turning to welcome Finn. They don't see her outside the circle of light.

"Hi, Chloe." Wy comes up behind her and puts his hands lightly on her waist, resting on the swell of her hips.

The bottoms of her feet tingle as she watches Finn. Wy's breath on her neck smells of beer and smoke. She's afraid again. She feels as if the demons from all the ghostly images she's seen are squirming under her skin. People struggling to stay calm as they're drawn slowly into the great magnetic ring of the MRI, like bodies on the conveyer belt to the crematorium. Their terror turned into a computer image. The radiologist ordering a change in frequency to bring the tumours into greater definition. Some of the white forms blooming in the brain stem they call angels.

Chloe now feels the great magnets struggle to pull all the ions in her cells into alignment. She resists the yearning of the iron in her blood. She wants to know what is hers alone, without Wy behind or Finn in front. But as she pauses there on the edge of the party, she is also afraid she is as empty as the clamshell in her pocket.

"I love your Cadillac, Wy."

"It's not entirely mine, Chloe. Where is it?"

"Stuck. Just this side of the spit."

"Waiting for its knight in shining armour?" Wy giggles. "With damp undies." They both laugh. Wy buries his nose in her neck. "Ah, vanilla air freshener."

"I threw it out the window."

He turns her around and kisses her forehead. "It's not a party without you. Everyone's been asking for you."

He pulls her into the light, leads her toward the food. Friends call to her, draw her into their warmth. She sparkles and flashes between the pots of steaming chowder, great iron skillets of halibut cheeks, alder racks of salmon tilting over glowing coals, through the clouds of smoke and the smell of salty sweat. She fills a plate. "Go play, Wy. I have serious work to do."

Instead he takes her plate and feeds her, first with a fork, next with his fingers, and then with his mouth.

"If anyone could make my ghosts go away, it'd be you, Sheriff," Chloe says.

Wy flips a chicken wing like a six-shooter and fires soft little pops at her belly and breasts. He blows imaginary smoke from the wing tip. "There. I got 'em."

Then he disappears, and Chloe feels as if she's alone on the beach. She gets up to dance, to empty her head, but the food has made her slow and the strain of the long trek pulls at her calf muscles. She sinks back down, closes her eyes, and tries to shut everything out.

⁂

Chloe is dozing when the drums stop and the voices fade into murmurs. From the darkness behind her, a violin begins, high and sweet in some ancient minor key. It hushes all human sounds. Chloe is surprised at her sudden jealousy. She has no talent like this, no voice to speak to each person alone yet link them all.

Shielding her eyes from the lights of a pickup roaring past her and out toward the spit, she sees Wy at the wheel, laughing with two other men. The Cadillac, she remembers. Wy is taking care of business. He can't help it, would never leave the thing to be swallowed by the sea. He will be fine with or without her, Finn has already forgotten her, and the gleaming steel tube awaits her in Vancouver. If she doesn't go back, what will she do? She may shine in reflected light, but she emits none of her own.

The tide is coming in and the waves lap at the lower fires. She shivers in the cold, feels like an echo of the girl: beginning trivial chores, dropping them, unravelling as everyone around has fun, has purpose.

The circle of dancers shifts in front of her. In its centre Finn stands still. As the fiddle picks up speed, he lifts his shoulders and expands his chest until he seems filled with the music. Filled to overflowing.

He begins to move and the circle makes way for him. Chloe watches, emptying herself into his movements. Whether he follows the music or it follows him is impossible to tell. He leaps and spins faster and faster, sending up arcs of phosphorescence from the rising water. When the violin finally slows, he curls into a crouch, turning so slowly it seems he must fall.

Chloe feels, as his powerful knees unbend, as he rises again, that he carries with him the great weight of all her cares. The music stops. He straightens, turns, and collapses into the shallows of the incoming tide.

In the hush Chloe hears the waves shiver off his body. As the cheering and applause begin, the girl slips down beside Chloe, offering her a blanket. Her frail shape and sharp edges remind Chloe of the hummingbird. She wraps them both in the blanket and they sit together, sharing heat and waiting for whatever comes next.

Shooting in the Dark

It was one of those end-of-August days. If the sun comes out, it could warm right up. If rain moves in, you'd want a down vest under your slicker. I was breaking my last duck egg over the first pine mushrooms of the season when I heard feet on the porch. It was, let me think, the fourth omelette I had made since I set the bread to rise at seven. By this time the bread was hot out of the oven and I was thinking maybe if I stayed quiet in the kitchen whoever it was would go away and let me eat in peace.

"Why won't your gate open?" A girl in the hall.

Frankie, my idiot son, hadn't bothered to close the door when he left, my last three eggs but one still stuck in his teeth. I beat the egg as it spread and bubbled through mushrooms and tomatoes, flipped the whole mess, and scooped it onto a piece of bread. "Truck backed into it. Buggered the latch."

"Mind if I come in?"

I felt her eyes on my back. I felt the T-shirt snug against the bulge at the waistband of my jeans, and I was mad for even thinking about it.

"You must be Chloe. Funny name that. Doesn't seem to know what to do with itself at the end there." I turned.

A little barefoot thing in hippie clothes hanging like wet kelp off tiny breasts and narrow hips. A limpet, for God's sake, strung onto her eyebrow ring. Like her shaved head was some kind of rock at low tide. And sure enough, when she turned to look around the usual mess of the place, I saw three barnacles wired up the side of one ear. And still cute as pie. The girlfriend.

"He's gone to the ferry to pick up a car. He'll be a while. You can wait if you want."

I tried not to gobble while she thought about it. Her feet squeaked on the linoleum. Must have started raining. "You are Chloe, aren't you?"

"Yeah, yeah. You're..."

"Bunny. Sit, why don't you? I've got to get some food in me. Then I'll make a cup of tea."

"Bunny?"

"Of Queen Charlotte Automobile Lease and Service Centre. Known locally as Bunny's Beaters. Wy's new business partner."

I knew what she was thinking. Looking around this kitchen. Shelves of preserves, two fridges, the freezer, bundles of herbs hanging from the ceiling rack. Dishes from too goddamn many breakfasts and last night's dinner piled in the sink. Jars of salmon on the washing machine.

"But this looks so..." Her hands fell.

The pinks were running, the pine mushrooms were rising in the bush, and the tourists were finally leaving Haida Gwaii. But not soon enough for me. I snarled, just a little. "You got a problem with a mechanic who can cook? Seems all most girls your age can do is microwave nachos and hitchhike."

"This was a big mistake. Just tell Wy I'll see him around."

I should have said okay. Let her go. Instead I said, "Keep your pantlets on. I just bark a little. Don't bite. As soon as the food kicks in, I'll be my usual cheerful self."

She hesitated.

"Besides, Wy will be pissed off at both of us if you're not here when he gets back."

"I'm supposed to tremble?"

"That's better. No cringing before boyfriends."

From somewhere behind me the phone rang.

"He's been close to moping since you told him you were going out on tonight's boat."

I found the phone under a stack of invoices on the dryer and listened to my son ask me a favour. "Yes, Frankie," I told him. "I'll try to get you one. I already told you. No, Tyler can't come with me. He does nothing but howl when his feet get wet, for Chrissakes."

I pulled the plate across the table and ate while he accused me of a lack of grandmotherly feelings. The girl filled the kettle and began clearing the dishes out of the sink. If you welcome people into your house, this kind happens along often enough. Someone who can't help but pick up a cloth and start wiping. Frankie's voice a whine inside my head wanting to unload his son into someone else's care. "I don't need anyone with me, and it's none of your business where I'm going."

I wouldn't have made her the type, but she knew what she was doing. Piled dirty glasses in the sink, squirted them with dish soap she found somewhere in the tangle, then ran hot water over it all.

"If I'm not here when you come by for breakfast tomorrow, ask Homer where I keep my will." I was tempted to unplug the phone, but I had three cars out on the road. It never pays. So I hung up and made the tea. "You don't have to do that," I told her, though I was glad someone was.

"I don't mind."

I felt old that morning. My knees ached as I sat back down. "Do you check in on your mother three times a day?" I asked her. "At least once in person?"

She laughed and poured the tea. "My mother paid a year's rent on our basement suite and moved to Toronto a month after I graduated from high school. She phones once a week when she's sure I'm not home and talks to the answering machine she gave me."

"Wow. Very impressive. If I had enough dough, I might try that. Except I have a daughter in Toronto. And one in Vancouver. A son in Kamloops and another in Courtenay. Where would I go?"

"I'd have thought Queen Charlotte City would be far enough."

"Me too. Until Frankie moved in right down the street."

"All these kids. Why do you need Wy?"

Ah. The boyfriend. Like it's my fault he's staying here instead of going back to Vancouver. It happens to all kinds. You're not sure why you stay but after a while it starts to feel like home. Or as close as you're ever going to get to one.

"I seem to prefer other people's children. I finally figured out why this morning, watching Frankie shovel those eggs into his mouth. My own remind me of their fathers."

Homer roared up then. Her face turned watchful until she heard his feet pound up the steps. Definitely not her light-footed boy.

"This is Chloe, Homer."

He yanked off his cap, wiped his forehead with his sleeve. Nodded toward her. Such a gentleman, even if he did sweat like a peasant.

"Wy's girlfriend."

She was pretty quick to set us straight. "We're going our separate ways, so I guess as of tomorrow, he doesn't have a girlfriend."

Homer looked bewildered. If they were fighting, why was she here? he asked me later. If not, why was she going? To her, he said nothing. "All those tires are coming in this afternoon, Bunny. You want me to go down and pick them up?"

I was happy for his help, as always, and packed a couple jars of salmon for him to drop with old Emma. Another woman pretty good at pissing off her kids.

The phone rang again. A rental out of gas on the Rennell Sound road. The driver unfortunately had a cell phone. Told me I should have warned him there weren't any gas stations on logging roads. The mud was awful and what about bears? By the time I calmed him down, Chloe had cleared enough away to be wiping the counters. I hadn't seen the colour of the arborite for weeks. An ugly yellow.

"Customers like that are why I need Wy," I told her. "I just piss them off. Give me axle grease any time. Now sit down, drink your tea, and eat some of Bunny's baking." I cut her a slice of bread.

And we did manage a few peaceful moments. You know how they surprise you? We were drinking mint tea and I was remembering floating down the Yakoun, letting the canoe drift close to the bank and gathering the mint, the smell filling the boat as I paddled down to the inlet. Outside, the neighbour's ducks quacked as if an eagle was looking down at them. A couple of dogs barked. The wind was picking up, soughing through the big cedars back of the house. When she broke through that, I got angry so fast I knew I needed some time alone.

"Did you ever think most of us would be better off without parents?" she asked me. "When I think about all the—no offence meant—fuckups."

I felt my hackles rise, like that old bitch of Emma's. "Mostly I think about how much my kids—bless the little feet they walk on—have, no offence meant, screwed up my life." I leaned in close, could smell her sweat. "And don't even start to talk to me about choice."

We were ready to tear right into something, but Wy showed up. Soaked, hair plastered to his head, standing on the mat, peeling off his anorak. "Hey, Chloe," he said, "kiss me now." Stuck out his chin, water dripping off his nose.

We joked back and forth a bit. He grabbed Chloe, kissed the top of her head, grinned at me. I remember that about him. Always figured he'd be welcome and he mostly was. But I could feel the strain. She was holding herself back, fingers wrapped around the mug, the other hand gathering and spreading bread crumbs on her plate. So I told him to take care of the empty gas tank and left them to sort out their day.

I thought that would be the end of it. Walking across to the shop, I went straight to the tool cupboard, unlocked it, and pulled out my rifle. I wasn't going to feel guilty about them splitting up. I didn't know Wy had a girlfriend when we talked about the business. He never said *we* when he spoke. Besides, no one at the tender age of twenty should be thinking long-term anything.

But she was a fool to give him up. I remember thinking that, remembered my first marriage. I showed Homer the picture, told him that guy shows up he never tells him where I am. He calls me first and then calls the cops. He's the reason I took up deer hunting in the first place. To practise killing something with beautiful brown eyes. So I'd be ready.

His parents should have been locked up with him—rich eastern bastards buying him off instead of seeing his craziness got taken care of. I still wake up sweating and cold to think he might find me, might show up on that ugly doormat and hold out his hand the way he used to. Like he was God and I was a crawling thing. His little crustacean, he'd call me. Saying it *crushtacean* or *curstacean*, depending on his mood. When I see a crab running for cover, or hungry folk crunching their shells with pliers, butter dripping down their chins, I remember that creep. There's parts of me that still ache from his attentions.

So I cleaned my rifle and got ready to bag a plump little deer. But my mean streak, the part that makes sure the most impatient tourist waits the longest for his car, that wishes Frankie would, well, disappear somehow, that part began to think it might be fun to cook up a mess of deer organs for the girlfriend. Probably a vegan. I'd be back in time to screw up the sexy farewell with blood and guts. See? I am not a nice person.

I made lots of noise when I went back into the kitchen just in case the sexy farewell had already started. She was looking through the binoculars at a kingfisher. Alone. Wy had gone to refill the car.

"There was this guy, a biologist up on Rose Spit," she said. "Spent most of the summer counting birds. Gives you a different perspective."

"Different than what?" I asked her. Damned if she didn't start twisting that bloody shell on her eyebrow. Made my stomach churn.

She shrugged. "To see the same thing day after day and not get bored. Get excited when there's a little change. Two birds come. Another goes."

"Paying close attention makes what's different stand out." I was thinking engines.

"How do you decide what to pay attention to?"

I couldn't answer. When my dad died, he left me all his tools. Holding them, placing my hands where his had been, brought me somehow into his company. Gave me the courage to gather up the kids and leave that bastard. So I became a mechanic.

"It just happens," I finally said. "Like it did for Wy. He's a natural business guy. Has that people magic."

"Wy." Her voice thickened. "Wy's problem is picking between the three million things he really wants to do. He's fun. His stuff is fun." She lifted the binoculars again. "But it isn't mine. I've been paying attention since he told me he was staying, and I'm not hearing anything telling me to stay too." The glasses followed a bird's flight. "Maybe my strength is indecision."

"Wow. That's going to be useful."

"Thank you. It hasn't been easy."

"I might be kidding."

"Like I didn't notice. But I'm not going to pretend. That's all."

I didn't realize it until later, but what she said kind of impressed me. I've always hated not knowing where I was headed. Hated it so much I decided my way in and out of three marriages and five children by the time I was thirty-five.

"Ever been hunting?" I asked her.

Her nose wrinkled. "No."

"Want to come?"

It stopped her. The refrigerator hummed. A car backfired. That tap, damn it, dripped. Still does.

"Why not?" she finally said. "It can't be any worse than this saying-goodbye stuff. He is so damned appealing."

"You're right there," I said, and you should have seen her eyes get sharp. Big grey eyes. Same colour as the shell. I laughed. "Believe me, when you get to be my advanced age, it's fun to look, but no one under fifty looks back. All those years you thought how great it would be if men would see you for who you really are and not for the shape of your legs or the heft of your boobs. But when they do, boy, it's a shock."

I rustled her up some of Tyler's black-and-yellow rain gear because it was going to be wet out in that drizzle.

"I feel like a bumblebee."

"You look like a Zodiac."

"Uninflated, I hope."

"I'll keep an eye on him for you."

"Huh?" She was bent, tucking her pants into the boots.

"Wy."

"Keep an eye on him?" She straightened. "Are you for real? You think I'm a flake, don't you? Not that it's any of your business what Wy does, or what I do, or what I feel about what he does, but you know, if you go, you go. You don't make the other person wait for you. That's just some kind of weird shit."

Her voice got high and breathy, dippy-bimbo style. "We've decided to live apart for a while, you know, and see what happens. To stay open to life's possibilities." She gagged. Made me laugh.

But driving through the drizzle, feeling like the inside of a rubber glove, I wished I was alone. When I'm alone, I don't notice how trashy this place gets. Muddy trucks coming back from the west coast, piled with dirt bikes and lawn chairs, dragging boats. The landings, a few stunted rusty trees poking through the gravel as packed and barren as concrete. And the bloody clearcuts. Gashes going on forever wherever you looked. The only graceful things were the deer I was planning to shoot.

"What's wrong with those ones?" she asked.

Three, four grazed in the ditch.

"I want to get off the main road. Don't like an audience much."

"So why am I here?"

I didn't answer because I was wishing she wasn't. You know that feeling when your mind is linked to this person beside you, wondering what they're thinking. Feeling. Not free to roam. I never learn.

I took the next side road, then turned again, inward like a spiral. The alders moved closer. It never takes long. Chloe saw one first and pointed. Head down at the bend ahead. I pulled over and turned off the engine, signalling for her to keep still as I opened my door.

Sliding out into the rain, I took the rifle from the rack, stepped away from the truck, and sighted. Chloe opened her door and I paused, half expecting her to yell. Scare it away. Her door brushed the alder, and the deer looked up at her. I squeezed and the cinnamon hair tufted where I had aimed. You know how the noise fills your head, the thud of the rifle against your shoulder? I can still hear it. Feel it. The deer took ten steps into the alder, then shivered to the ground. Chloe ran toward it.

"Stop!" I yelled. I was fierce. She stopped suddenly. "Leave it in peace."

Her startled face, a white smear above the raincoat. "In peace?"

"I have my reasons. You wait."

She looked scared, and I realized the rifle was still pointing. I lowered it, knowing I looked crazy. Feeling excited and like crap both at once. Happens every time.

When I feel like that, I don't want to see the eyes glaze, the muscles jerk under the wet hair. Don't get me wrong. It's not guilt. I was going to eat that deer, and hunting deer makes more sense here than slaughtering cows. I can't bear to think of a cow's life, its plodding stupidity.

It's respect. Twitching and cooling into stillness. I'd like to be alone when that happens to me. I want to pay attention to my own dying, not think about my kids squabbling, worry about how they're feeling. I get tired of guessing what people feel and making the daily adjustments so they'll feel better. I wanted to let the deer die in the privacy of its own self, not with me and my knife hovering over it.

The moment passed. A squirrel chattered insanely. A jay floated into the trees above the deer. I gathered my gear and walked over to it. "It's okay now."

Chloe was right beside me when I nudged the deer. "That would depend on whose opinion you asked," she said.

I lifted a leg, let it drop. It coiled back toward the belly as it fell. A nice little doe.

"Those hooves look dangerous."

"They are. Little knives. You don't want to start anything until the animal's well and truly dead."

I got to work. Slit the throat and drained the blood into the gravel. Chloe surprised me.

"This'll be interesting. We don't get much real anatomy. Pictures and models. Computer images."

"What are you talking about?"

"Hasn't Wy told you I'm going back to school?"

"No. He said you were going back to Vancouver. Couldn't decide if you wanted to stay, so you thought you'd go. Didn't you say something about indecision?"

"Not making a decision is a kind of choosing, I guess. I haven't withdrawn, and if I get back to Vancouver before the first day of classes, I'll probably go."

"What is it? Nursing?"

"Radiology. X rays. MRI. Brain scans. That kind of thing. I thought Wy would have mentioned it. I've already done one year. Doesn't matter."

It did though. She drooped a little. No matter how much any of us pretends, we all want to be the centre of someone's universe. As I spread the legs, she stroked the warm, white belly.

"Hold this, will you? Just above the hoof."

She squatted in the damp grass and gripped the ankle.

I cut. Anus to sternum. Heat steamed into the cool air. The guts bulged. I reached inside, cut the membrane away from the rib cage, and sat back as the hot coils spilled onto the grass. God, there's a lot of heat inside a mammal's body. When you're out in the cold and wet like that, the heat scalds you.

"The peritoneum," she said, still holding the leg but talking through her nose, trying not to smell. "The esophagus," she said as I cut it. She looked away as I sliced around the anus, freeing the viscera.

As we lifted the body onto the tarp, away from the guts, she slipped in the bloody gravel.

"I hate this place," she said, climbing to her feet. "The inside of this place. The beaches are beautiful, most of them, except for that disgusting mud hole below Charlotte. But the damp mouldy God-for-fucking-saken green gloom—I am so sick of it. I'm looking forward to pavement." Blood streaked one cheek. Mud smeared her left shoulder.

"Your city friends might think twice about welcoming you if they saw you now."

She drew the back of her hand across her forehead, smearing water and blood, and giggled. "Natural-born killer. When you see blood and guts spurting all over the screen, you never think about how bad it must smell."

That giggle made me shiver. You know all the talk about witches? How women arrive on island in twos and threes, disappear into the bush, and come out with wild eyes. Stories about full-moon rituals, fires, and dances on the beach. Sculptures the tide takes away. Sacred places.

I looked through the dripping alder to the gravel road a few yards away. An old fuel drum rusted under some rain-blackened nettles. Blue oil containers in the ditch. Black plastic tangled in frayed cable. We're so dumb. Any place—some parking lot, the dump, for God's sake—could be one of those special places they talk about. And we'd toss our old refrigerator right on top of it and walk away, glad to be rid of a noisy motor and rusting wire shelves.

Looking at that blood-smeared girl who knew how to use those big humming machines that see inside people's sick bodies, I knew for certain that not very many of us have any kind of clue about what we're messing with as we stumble through our days.

"You're not some kind of witch, are you?"

Her eyes opened wide. "What?"

"You look pretty wild, you know."

"You don't look so downtown yourself."

"Actually, you look like a flaky piece of fluff at a primal-scream therapy workshop."

"Fuck you too. You look like what my mother calls white trash with a hankering for dirt bikes."

We were both laughing, the deer steaming between us.

"I used to live in Vancouver, you know," I said. "When you walked in this morning, I took you for one of those Commercial Drive girls who live on cappuccino."

"And vegan burgers. I know. I am one of those Commercial Drive girls, but I prefer samosas." She sniffed, still trying not to smell. "What about you? Don't you have any hankerings to smear yourself with blood and dance naked? Make offerings to the goddess?"

"Well, I like to eat fresh heart and liver. Sometimes I bring my Coleman stove out with me and cook it up right there."

Damned if she didn't stick the liver on the tip of my knife. "Don't want to try it raw?"

I didn't, though I know some who do. I passed her the Tupperware to stash it for later.

That girl was efficient. She pulled when I said pull. The skin slid off easy, and there was that funny moment when all mammals start to look human. Hairless meat, still warm, rippling as the nerves cooled. But she kept going. She steadied the legs when I quartered the meat. She held the head and whispered to it as I sliced it off. She helped me lift the meat onto the ice in the box in the back of the pickup.

It wasn't until we were washing up that she lost it. She shook her hands dry, then smelled them. Back in the bush, the jay settled onto the head and went after the eyes.

Without any fuss she walked into the trees and threw up. Her face was so white the little bit of blond hair she had showed up almost green. She gulped some water, spit, then crossed her arms on the rim of the pickup box, lay down her head, and cried.

The girl was such a mess she needed a pressure wash, for God's sake. I tried to clean her up with some paper towels. Dabbing at the blood and tears on her face, I felt the tender feeling you get when you hear the total despair of a five-year-old crying. Until she opened her mouth.

"Even this," she snivelled. "I help off a poor fucking deer because I want to make a point. Prove something to you. I don't even know you. To Wy. I want him to get back and be mad because I'm not there. Or sad. Something. I don't want him to think I'm waiting for him."

I packed up everything.

"I spent three days camping after he came down here. Assert my independence. Not be his little satellite."

I poured her some tea and bundled her into the truck. She kept talking. "I met this guy on the beach, this biologist."

"The one with the binoculars."

"Yeah, him. He'd spent four months basically alone. Happily. And I can't stand three days in my own company, three days trying not to think because my own thoughts bore me to fucking tears."

I don't know which is worse. Too much self-doubt or not enough. She probably slept with the guy to prove something too. Felt guilty and was mad about feeling guilty. At least she was still a baby. Not like my Frankie, who's spent thirty years blaming other people for his failings.

"He might have been pining after his girlfriend the whole summer for all you know," I told her. "You might be able to see inside people's heads with those fancy machines, but you can't see what they're thinking."

She blew her nose.

"You can be useful though. Help people get better."

"The machine can help. The doctor can help. I just run the equipment."

"Crap. When you're sick or hurt and that person running the machines is kind, it makes all the difference."

I had to stop there. If I'd been asked to pick someone who'd make me think, the last person I'd have chosen would be a girl like Chloe. But she was pressing all my buttons. From thirty, thirty-five years ago came this face, this tender woman with bright lipstick and too much makeup bending over me as she arranged my arm and shoulder on the X-ray table. The same shoulder in which I could still feel the rifle's recoil. She had tears rising. She knew how much it hurt. I was whispering, afraid that husband of mine would somehow hear me. "It's nothing," I said. "I'm just clumsy."

"You get him in here one time, honey, and I'll turn on the radiation and walk away for my coffee break. When I come back, he'll think twice about pulling this kind of stunt."

Her voice. It was one of those whiskey voices. Must have smoked. Whimpering crustacean that he'd named me, I didn't walk away that time. But hers was the first whisper in the world's silence.

Neither of us said anything more until we drove up to my busted gate.

"Toss those duds in the washer so the blood doesn't get caked on," I said. "Hose down the boots. Tyler'd kill me if he knew I lent them out."

"What about you?"

I could see Wy moving around in the kitchen and didn't feel like watching his sorrow. "I've gotta drop off the meat with Frankie's wife, help Homer with those tires. Probably go for a drink after. See you sometime."

"Yeah. Maybe. Thanks, I guess." She climbed down from the cab, and her right pant leg slid up. A smear of blood dribbled down her leg. I told her. She didn't look back. "Yeah. I know. I can always feel it begin. Just my luck."

I dropped off the meat and went to see Emma. She's the one I blubber to. She was sitting in her chair by the window looking out across the strait. Had the fire going. I fixed her some salmon, boiled a potato. Told her about the hunt.

She didn't like that part about the girl bleeding–said the meat would be unclean. When I told her Frankie had it already, she shook her head. Won't hurt him, she said. But she made me feed the liver to the dog, right there.

"There's some say women shouldn't hunt," she said. "I don't go along with that. But you've got to know what you're doing."

She didn't say anything else. I didn't ask. Seems none of us know what we're doing anymore. Now I only fire the rifle to scare the ravens out of my huckleberries.

Hecate Strait

The boy slows his truck beside me on the road. I grip my dog's collar. He asks me the way to the mountains.

For what kind of journey? I ask.

A hike, he says.

A fast, steep climb, a gentle grade, a circle, a coming and a going?

I need to know all this before I set out?

You already have set out.

He shifts into gear. I put one hand on the door frame.

Why are you going?

To think, he says. To think and sweat.

I have wood that needs splitting.

Alone.

I have only one axe, I say. Then tell him the way to a lake. A hard climb. His thighs resting on the seat look sturdy. His arms would have shredded my woodpile.

What's your name? I ask.

Finn.

His voice is rough. Unused to speech. It's risky to hike alone in these mountains, and he sounds as if he's been too much alone already.

Stop by on your way out. I point to my house. So I know you're safe.

Okay.

I'll give you tea.

All right.

I release the dog to chase the truck around the bend.

I read poetry when the short heat of summer leaches into September frosts. *What misery to be afraid of death.* In my kitchen overlooking an ancient gully where seasons rise and subside, I tamp mint leaves into a tea ball. The clay cup warms my hand. I am a visitor here in spite of thirty years. *What wretchedness, to believe only in what can be proven.* I am alone.

Every morning before I make my tea, I get dressed. I brush my hair, clean my teeth, and make my bed. Always. I am afraid of falling into slovenliness as my hips stiffen, my knees ache. I struggle to think my own thoughts. When I manage equilibrium in their swirling midst, my body becomes a place where peace enters.

Travellers to the mountains often stop at my door for directions. The calm surface of my tea reflects their distractions. Their internal compasses have been damaged by competing magnetic fields. You may dislike this metaphor. The rancher does. He spits at his blue heeler's feet.

There's trails everywhere, he says. Who needs to know which way is north?

His cattle know more about the earth's turning than he does. They know some trails lead through fog to the cliff's edge. Others lead into the stockyard's truck.

I tie the dog and walk into town. When I pick up my mail, I hear a young couple laughing over postcards. They have come from a summer in the bush and are returning to the city. Battered boots. Thick socks. Brown muscular calves, thighs disappearing into ragged shorts. Layers of cotton, vests, sweaters trapping the scent of their bodies. The girl's naked shoulder bright through a rip. To them I am invisible.

At the fruit truck I resist the seduction of artichokes and buy pears and peppers. Tonight I will eat the peppers. The pears will ripen in the blue bowl.

Evenings I sit outside on my bench, a worn fir plank on lichened stone. Brandy melts the ice in my glass. The dog lies behind my ankles. I look beyond my garden. The bushes that screen me brighten in the sun's setting, in the summer's passing. The rancher drives up. He whistles at the dog. He doesn't believe the dog is deaf and wants to trick him into forgetting the charade. The dog smells the blue heeler on his boots and draws back his muzzle.

Like the lord of the neighbouring manor, the rancher comes at the beginning of every month to question me. He dreams of merging our estates.

I am too old, I tell him. I cannot marry anyone.

He wouldn't be happy with me. He doesn't believe my dog is deaf because the dog has the trick of attentiveness, of clever second-guessing. He thinks that I, too, know more than I let on. He does not understand that I am no more than a conduit, a way point between the mountains and the sea, between the bush and the city, between the world and dreaming. Tides that rise and fall many mountain ranges from here echo in my blood.

I wait until he's gone to go inside. To wander the shadows of my house, trace dust on a bookshelf, watch grass tremble in the clay pot when a diesel passes. To pour another drink, put on a shawl, and step back outside into darkness. The creek's low murmur filters through the silence between trucks. The spicy smell of evening-scented stock pools and eddies in the cooling air. I sit and sip and smell and listen.

There is a man I would marry. He guides fishermen down near the mouth of the river. When I close my eyes, I see him bending to remove the hip waders, see them outline the curve of his buttocks. He doesn't like my cows and complains when the rancher accompanies them down to my fields.

I close my eyes and try not to measure the time since his last departure. When I smell salt, I think it is him. But the song I hear is thin, distant, a song being sung over water in a high place. A song the creek is carrying down to the sea. I do not understand the words, but I recognize the voice. It is the boy.

⁂

Finn learned silence as a child sitting, knees pulled to his chest, in the jumble of chair and human legs under the kitchen table. It was there he'd heard his mother's confessions, his father's silence. Later he'd been happiest curled up in the shade under the front porch. Fathers mowed grass to release the ancient pleasure of cut fodder into suburban air. His mother's marigolds added their acid. Dried urine where the boys urinated, and their father, too, when he stayed out on the porch all night, drinking into the coolness that surfaced toward morning.

Finn found a spidery comfort there. The clatter of feet striped by slats of green light and shade emphasized his solitude. Into this peace he learned to hum songs that blended with the sound of the wooden lawn swing clacking, balls bouncing on the sidewalk, sprinklers, mothers talking over fences, uncles calling out of rolled-down car windows.

Oh, salamander, he hummed. Climb on my arm. Spider, leave me room or I will tear your web. Of the green mould that grew in the dampness, he asked forgiveness for the gouging of his knees and elbows.

Finn hums this porch song beside the alpine lake. He didn't know about mountains—how they loom at night, how they stretch you out in offering to the glittering stars. He comforts himself with thoughts of the lake draining into the creek. The woman's woodpile. The creek tumbling into the river, the river slipping through the mountains down to the ocean, the wide waters of the ocean lifted up by the shallows of Hecate Strait and spilled against the sandy eastern shore of Haida Gwaii. Where the solace of green silence returned to him, where almost everywhere recalled the space beneath his mother's porch.

⁂

The worn sheets on my bed feel like the skin on the fisherman's inner thighs. I leave my window open to let in the rise and fall of the creek.

⁂

On the deck of the ferry crossing Hecate Strait from Prince Rupert to Skidegate back in the spring, Finn failed to pinpoint the moment land disappeared. Before that day he had never seen the ocean. Now he couldn't see the shore. He heard the throb of the great diesel engine below decks and smelled its exhaust. He smelled grease from the kitchen, grease as heavy as the layers of paint covering the steel hull.

He sat on the grey deck and looked through the wire mesh of the railing. The sky was grey. The horizon was grey. The water far below was grey, spilling white where the hull sliced through it. He put his forehead against the mesh and imagined himself plunging down in the endless fall of the earth's turning.

⁂

I awaken to the sound of the dog's claws on the tiles. It walks across to the rug and sinks down with a pleasured groan. The nights are once again pitch. The moon, new.

⁂

Finn stretched flat, the metal cold against his thighs, his groin, his chest. The groan of the boat shuddering through the water increased his fear.

Is the great goddess of the underworld making you sick?

He rolled over and looked up. A girl lying on the life-jacket locker, her head propped on her elbow, blond hair tangled.

I didn't get that.

Hecate. The protector of witches, of sailors and hunters. The crone mother. The queen of the crossroads. Did you leave her offerings when you set out on your journey?

I seem to remember drinking too much.

Ah. Not good. Not respectful of the journey.

That was a week ago. In Toronto.

She has a long memory. Are you going to throw up?

I'm not sure. I'm trying to concentrate on not throwing up.

A bare foot dangled off the edge of the locker. The girl kicked it up and down.

Sometimes distraction works better than concentration, she said. Here's a riddle. It's a word that everybody knows. Hungry ends in *gry*. Angry ends in *gry*. What's the third word in the English language?

She stretched until both her feet arched. Finn drifted into spinning lists of words. Languor, he thought. Buggery. Gingery. Gingerly. Pedigree. Filigree.

⁂

I surface through watery light. Sun filtering through the willow leaves outside my window. Ophelia. *There's rosemary, that's for remembrance; pray, love, remember: and there is pansies, that's for thoughts.* The fisherman is not here and the sun will not yet have risen over the rock wall above the dreaming boy.

⁂

It was on Rose Spit that Finn recovered his childhood gift of silence. The long tail of sand rose from the waters of Dixon Entrance and Hecate Strait into the ragged rump of land. Great heaps of drift logs began the anchoring of shifting sand dunes. Prickly grass and wind-blasted pines continued the restless transformation. Behind the dunes the wind and water sounds dropped into the shelter of an earthbound world: mosses, lichens, spruce, cedar, and hemlock. The light changed, the smells changed, and he heard songbirds far back where the red huckleberries ripened.

He learned the names of plants and what they spoke of. If the poor settlers who'd tried to make a life here on what came to be called the Argonaut Plains had paid attention, a forester told him, they'd have known that all this lushness thrived in poor, very wet soil. Acid. Hopeless for crops.

Paid attention to what? Finn wondered. What clues signalled scarcity in the midst of all this green? When one of the huge cedars dropped, its torn roots exposed grey mineral soil. Finn sifted some through his fingers. He turned to the sunlight streaming through the opening in the canopy, stood with it full in his face, then dropped to lie facedown in its warmth beside the fallen tree. *Coptis asplenifolia* tickled his face. Fern-leaved goldthread.

He pressed against the damp moss until he felt the ground everywhere. He imagined himself the cedar log; alive enough to feel the sap slowing, pooling as its life drained away. He felt his restlessness ebb into stillness.

He'd gone somewhere that day he didn't recognize at first. He didn't know how happy he was until he felt the tiny claws of a chickadee in the hair curling at his neck. A presence like the salamanders under his childhood porch.

The dog whines at the door. It shoots out to bark at the dark shape bending a branch of the apple tree. The dog stops. The branch breaks, tumbling the bear to the grass. The bear runs for the bush. Tires squeal on the road beyond. I close the door. I do not want to hear a thud. Rosemary, I think. Today I must pick apples and make rosemary jelly.

In the high morning frost, Finn crawls out of his tent. He shivers and urinates, steam in the bitter air. His footprints are stained purple. He crouches. *Vaccinium caespitosum.* He picks one tiny berry and tastes it. Sweet and crystalline. He eats.

Above him the rock face still blocks the morning sun. Shadows move toward brightness, sending stones skittering into the lake. Finn looks, but not high enough. He is looking for bears. Not the *Ursus americanus carlottae* of Haida Gwaii. His hands are stained purple with berries. His lips are blue. *Ursus horribilis.* Grizzly. Even as the sun breaks free of the rock, menace enters the shadows.

I fill the sink with cold water and float apples. The knife snug against my finger, I cut away the bruises. The cracks where skin meets fingernail darken with the fruit's acid. The kettle fills quickly. The morning traffic blocks the sound of the creek.

I'm a biologist, Finn would tell hikers to Rose Spit. I'm counting things. Plants, birds.

Lonely? one girl asked.

You'd be surprised how many people pass through.

He found himself hiding like an uneasy bear. *Hungry.* Watching for the girl from the ferry. Avoiding the others.

My kitchen fills with the sweetness of apples. Their perfume steams my cold morning windows. Their juice a repository for stronger flavours.

Finn looks for a way up. The rock face splinters and slips down to scree, the scree crumbles to soil, and crusty lichens give reluctant way to heather and alpine willow. He memorizes a route that may bring him to the shoulder of the peak and begins to climb.

I scoop the cooked apples into a jelly bag and suspend them over a glass bowl. The juice drips a blush into the bowl's transparency. In a northern garden it would have been bear's tongue that led Eve to contemplate the apples clustered above her as she lay suspended in his articulation.

On Haida Gwaii, Finn began to dream of feet. The ferry girl's. Heels rubbed smooth and hard by sand, insteps arching into shadows he'd like to lick. Once, in his sleeping bag tucked under a tangle of drift logs, he felt a tremor move through the logs. Someone walking. Her toes stretched and contracted above him as she gauged the leap to the next log. She jumped and moved on, leaving him awake and erect. *Hungry.*

He scrambled into the bright air, compact, dishevelled, hairy—a bear spurting into speed and grace, running to the top of the dunes. The line of driftwood stretched trackless into the distance. He didn't know where his dream ended. He wanted to bellow her name. *Angry.* He didn't know what it was. The third word.

I bury what's left of the crushed apples deep in my compost, careful of bears. I don't want any more of their blood on my hands. The rancher rides out among his cows and mine, swatting their flanks, checking their udders, shooting coyotes and bears. He drops by to report. Blames wild animals for every death. Marauders, he calls them. He measures my doorway for his big frame, looks at the shoes scattered beside the door for the fisherman's. The rancher would never trust a man who lived off wild things, who didn't raise what he killed, who didn't kill what he caught.

⁂

Struggling up the scree, Finn pushes hard to drive blood to his arms and legs. It is cold in the shadow, and he wears only the T-shirt he slept in, his boots and jeans. When he traverses the slope, he sees tracks and porkpie hats of dung. He scoops it up. Sniffs. *Oreamnos americanus.* Mountain goats.

⁂

My black dog sniffs the gatepost at the bottom of the driveway, the place where all nighttime visitors deposit greetings, gossip, warnings. The paint has flaked off leaving grey wood as soft and exposed as my heart this morning. *The heart is three bowls always full and one empty,* I think. *The heart is a full set of goatprints.* I don't look down the road where the bear would have crossed.

⁂

Augury, Finn first thought when the ferry girl came to him again, her car stuck in the sand below the high-tide mark, her tangled hair shorn. He walked back along the beach with her, enjoying the compression of air between them as they moved together, moved in and out of the semiconsciousness of long-distance walking. Wondering if she'd remember the ferry, the riddle. When she didn't, he let the beach party claim him. Let the music swallow him.

⁂

I open my door. Two men my age. Hikers. The big one stops in the doorway and sucks in the smells: coffee and cooked apples.

The smaller man, the tidy one, speaks. The fellow at the gas station said you might be able to help us.

I invite them in. Offer coffee or mint tea. Behind them on the porch, a girl. Tiny. Blond. A shell threaded onto an eyebrow ring. Bare feet. She nods her head to tea.

We've just finished the most marvellous trip to the Charlottes, the neat man says.

Haida Gwaii, his partner corrects.

We aren't ready to break the spell. To return to the city. We asked about these mountains. They said to talk to you.

Can you recommend a trail, just a few hours, nothing too tough?

Nowhere you can go without at least good running shoes. I point to the girl's feet.

The Nepalese walk the Himalayas in bare feet. Her voice chimes.

Isn't she the silliest? We met her on the ferry. Hitchhiking to the city.

I describe a soft trail, one that crosses the shady back of a mountain. You turn around whenever you want. You can't get lost. There's nowhere to walk but on the trail.

If you wear shoes, the girl says, the whole world is made of leather. Then asks if she can eat a pear.

They're not ready, I tell her.

⁂

The climb has become steeper than he likes, but Finn wants to see goats. He creeps onto the shoulder of the rock face, expecting to see an expanse of some kind. An alpine meadow. But the mountains are tricksters. The shoulder is narrow, a heap of shattered rocks and a pathway into air. The goat tracks disappear over its edge. He hears clattering far below on rocks shrouded in the sudden fog rolling into the ravine and boiling up toward him. It blocks the sun and chills the sweat on his back. He turns, looks back down to his camp where the morning sun is transforming the frost to steam. A dark humped shape rises out of the small trees beside his tent and sniffs the air. Then the fog rears up and envelops him in shivering greyness. He hears nylon ripping.

Finn has seen bears cracking mussels on the beaches of Haida Gwaii. He has hidden himself among cedars and watched them on the banks of the Hiellen River. The only time they interfered with him was the time he walked with the ferry girl along the beach. Distracted from the remnants of a careless meal.

He laughed when he returned to his camp and saw the demolition. He sympathized with the bear. She'd finally discovered the food cache that had been under her nose all summer. All summer the girl had been there, just down the beach. Chloe. Finn had let his desire slip away. The bear had not.

The fog rolls back, and Finn sees the grizzly tossing his sleeping bag in the air, nosing it, shredding it.

Only days ago Finn counted stars on the beach near Tlell, gathering himself to enter the human world, to leave the green shadow of the islands. He was wrapped in his sleeping bag under a drift of logs when he felt a tremor. A dark shape blocked the stars, paused, gauged the gap in the logs above him. Dream taught, bear taught, he grabbed one ankle. She gasped, shook her foot. He held on.

Chloe.

Please let go.

You did this once before. Weeks ago.

She recognized him and stood still.

Or else I dreamt it. He squirmed out of his sleeping bag, still holding her ankle, and stood up. His face at her knees. She was wearing a dress. It rippled in the air. He felt the tendon slip across her ankle as she tightened her foot to jump. *Angry*? he asked.

It shifted back as she relaxed. Laughed. From the ferry, right? I forgot about that. Weird. Have you figured it out?

Not yet. I'm still working on it. His other hand took her foot and lifted it toward his face.

Hey! She put her hands on his shoulders to balance. He rubbed his cheek along the insole, over the heel.

This foot would make a track like the scoop of an abalone, he said, and waited.

She said nothing. Her breath on his face.

His hand moved up over the ankle to the shinbone.

Driftwood, an anchor for sand.

He brushed the hair where it thickened over her shin.

Plants finding enough stable ground to begin colonization. *Poa macrantha*. Dune bluegrass. *Carex arenicola*.

His fingers curled over her knee.

Your bones are the structure used to anchor muscle, skin.

His fingers moved behind her knee.

The soft lee, shelter.

As he kissed the place, his other hand released her ankle and slid up her thigh. He felt her muscles bunch, ready to leap. He looked up into the darkness. Her eyes flickered.

Angry? he asked.

She stepped across, straddling the gap. She wore nothing under the dress.

Adiantum pedatum, he said. Maidenhair fern. *Philonotis fontana. Agrostis aequivalvis*.

Hungry, she said.

And in that moment he understood why the early settlers stayed too long in the shaded bogs of the Argonaut Plains.

⁂

Why do you let them all come? the fisherman asked. In the early summer he had brought me a sign. PRIVATE DRIVE. His hands moved over my body.

The directions in the guidebooks aren't clear, I told him. The trails are confusing. They want to talk to someone who's walked them, they want to be sure.

Nothing is sure. His mouth at my breast.

I'd rather help them first than open the door at 3:00 a.m. to someone raving and lost. Broken collarbones.

My nipples tingled and rose up.

I think of them as mine.

He looked up. His mouth left a dark stain on my shirt. The travellers?

No. The mountains.

You take this too seriously. Come fishing.

⁂

Finn had forgotten these smells. He stood and snorted into the cold air. He rubbed his hands through his beard and hair. Sand stuck to his thighs. She was underneath his sleeping bag. One foot had slipped out, brown and smooth in the early light. He moved away so his erection would subside enough to let him urinate. The sand darkened and rivulets formed as his heat steamed into the morning.

He walked into the freezing ocean. He swam until he could barely feel his body, just the line of temperature where air met water. He hung, suspended in that line, and looked out across Hecate Strait. Grey to the black line of horizon beyond which the continent lay, waiting.

When he returned, he shook himself like a bear rising from a salmon stream, joyful after good fishing. He sprang up the beach to find his sleeping bag still warm. But empty.

⁂

I feel responsible, I told the fisherman. Their fears are my children. They require my tending.

He looked over my shoulder and out the window to the apples still young on the tree. My heart paused in its beating. *The heart is snowbound broken rock in the locked ribs of a man in the sun on the shore of the sea...* He did it gracefully as he did all things, but he was soon gone. The bones from the salmon he'd brought still unburnt.

⁂

Finn is cold. His T-shirt has dried into stiffness and the wind only stops against his bones. The fog swirls through the ravines and gullies surrounding him. In its shifting he sees the bear is still there. He envies it its fur rippling across powerful muscles. His camp turns into gaudy tatters of nylon, polypropylene, plastic: garbage. He is ashamed and afraid.

⁂

The jelly foams in the deep pot. Into each hot jar I drop a sprig of rosemary and three mint leaves. The dark greens brighten as I pour the golden liquid over the leaves. I wipe the rims, then tilt liquid wax to pool on liquid apple and drop a tiny flower in the centre. The pansies that grow wild in my yard. The wax thickens at the edges and sets its seal on summer. The jars tinkle when I slide them into rows.

⁂

The fog reveals one slope, then another. Between are secrets. Finn is hungry and stiff. He paces, kicks rocks over edges. He doesn't care about the bear anymore. He is ready to slide whooping down into its embrace, anything to be off the ridge. Then the sound of a bell rises from the other side. He peers down. A trail is suddenly visible. A pale line on a rocky cliff face disappearing on either side into forest.

He looks for a route, untutored in the way cliffs hide themselves in foliage, in the way ravines lose dimension and become one with the trees they divide. A shaded gully of snow anchored between boulders suddenly looks navigable. He laces up his boots tightly and steps onto the snow. He digs in one heel. The other. The angle of the slope is deceptive. He begins to slide.

⁂

My land spans the junction of three roads. One road dwindles into a rough track into the mountains. Another leads to town–to mail, domestic chores, mousetraps, and dog food. The third passes neat fields and abandoned hay barns on its way to the main highway between the coast and the city.

My summer-bred cows wander hills rich with browse. The winter hay is in the barn. My firewood waits. The garden cools the roots of vegetables, hardens them for winter. The leaves on my stripped apple tree curl in defeat, angry at my theft, like the bees I gave away so stricken was I in the face of their fury. Sting me, I told them. Anyone who conducts such thievery deserves it. In the remembered pain of their response, I feel a jolt as if someone is crying out. I cover my ears.

⁂

Finn's fall carries him across the trail into the thin branches of a mountain ash. He crashes to the base of the tree and tries to make sense of the roar rising like great waves in his ears. With it comes darkness, though he knows his eyes are open. He feels a scratch where his eyelid rubs across his cornea.

⁂

I take off my shoes as the afternoon shadows stretch across the garden. The whole world is made of leather, the girl said. Daily, I walk across this ground on the backs of my cows. My fruit kills bears. My garden distracts deer from their rightful pursuits. The soles of my feet are as white as their lifted tails. The planks of the deck are still warm from the sun.

I walk inside to arrange jelly jars in a basket for the root cellar. The tiles are cold. I feel the grit of spilled sugar beside the stove. Outside on the grass I suddenly remember a child running beneath fruit trees, air on her skin, arms spread wide, jubilant in her naked escape into a yard at the edge of a forest hundreds of miles from here. Purple plums smeared on my mouth. My feet tough little paws as familiar with every outside texture of earth and pavement as a cat's.

⁂

Finn thinks the fog has moved inside his head. He is afraid he will lose his footing. He flexes one foot. The ground moves so strangely it takes him time to realize the boot is pressing against a loose stone. The stone moves and he does not. Slowly he feels gravity's embrace, its pressure along an unfamiliar axis. He is not standing; he is crumpled on his left side, his face pushed into dead leaves. He turns his head to find the sky, and pain brings the darkness again.

⁂

The surefooted memory dissolves as my feet step onto the path to the root cellar. All the weight of my body is expressed in their shrinking from sharp points of gravel. The weight of a human body is a serious burden, they tell me as I hobble to the door into the hillside.

⁂

He hears bells and wonders if he's dead. They come closer. He sees boots above him on the trail and tries to cry out, but his mouth is full of leaves. He sees more boots and the bell moves past him. Then he sees a foot lifting, a bare foot, a bruise flowering on the instep where he bit too hard. He spits leaves against the rising waves.

Chloe, he calls. Chloe.

The foot pauses and turns on the narrow path.

⁂

In the dimness I see the cabbages already wrapped, the jars of peaches, the purple plums floating. Spiderwebs in my hair. The dog's tail stirs up dust in the doorway. I feel as if all the weight of my preserves, my house, my cows, my land is on my shoulders and driving down into the pale soles of my tender feet. I back into the sunlight, bringing the golden jelly with me. I cannot bear to leave it behind in darkness. I kick the door shut, my heel hard against the rough splinters. My bones ache.

⁂

Don't touch me, he whimpers as the three slide down beside him.

The small man's hands move over his body, gentle, knowledgeable. It's okay. We're not going to move you. He sits back on his heels. Now, tell me your name.

Finn tells him.

And can you tell me how you got quite so bent up slipping off the path? The man is stripping off his jacket and beckoning the others to give him what extra clothing they have.

Finn tells him his fall began farther up. The man pauses in his arrangement of fleeces and T-shirts around Finn to look. There is silence, then a low whistle from the other man.

We can't move you until we get help. I need you to promise not to move your head. Not at all.

No problem, Finn says. I tried once. That was enough.

⁂

I'm lying on the deck soaking up the last of the sun's heat when the rancher drives up. His feet on the steps send reverberations through the planks under my back. My dog snarls at the blue heeler in the cab of his pickup.

He is dark against the sun. I squeeze my eyes together to dissolve the blur. Your feet are dirty, he tells me as I struggle into a sitting position. I pull one foot toward my belly and look. Grass, clay from the root cellar. And cold, I say, getting up.

About my cows, I begin.

Plenty of feed up there for another month, he says.

I've been thinking about selling the herd.

All of them? He is alert to possibilities.

I'm not sure yet. I need to get away for a while.

He sets his hat back on his head and looks at the shoes tumbled at the doorway.

Why would you want to leave now? The bugs are gone, the underbrush is thinning out, and the bears are mostly down fishing. Or trying to get there.

I have seen the ravens gathering and stop him from talking about the one dead beside the road. I tell him I'll be in touch.

⁂

I raise the axe and bring it down on rounds of pine. I name my cows and conjure up their faces. The wood splits cleanly. I am wet with sweat when the big hiker drives up. He runs to me without any wasted moves, without panic.

We found a kid beside the trail. He fell. I need to phone for help.

Where? I ask as we go inside.

Finn, I say when he describes him. How did he get there?

He was trying to come down that slope.

He didn't look that stupid.

How long will it take them to get here?

Couple more minutes. You okay? You need anything?

A drink of water maybe. He gulps it by the sink, looking down into my gully. Those guys, will they know what they're doing?

Yes.

⁂

What is the third word? Finn is in the hospital. He has broken various bones in his left side: ribs, collarbone, scapula.

Chloe takes her feet off the bed, looks out at the mountain filling the window. It's stupid, she says.

A word everyone knows, you said. Like *angry*. Like *hungry*. He is stubborn.

The third word in the English language.

What is it?

Language. That's the third word in the English language.

Language?

The is number one, *English* is number two, *language* is number three. I told you it was stupid.

He is not angry. His disappointment is emptiness.

⁂

I won't be able to manage that woodpile, Finn tells me. The girl, Chloe, it seems, is gone.

He asks about the bear, the mess it left beside the lake.

I peel him a pear. It's taken care of, I say, handing him slices. Not a trace of you remains. And the bear has moved on.

He swallows. Why are you here?

I sent you on that trail.

The trail did me no harm.

I know. It's the space between trails that causes difficulties.

He nods. He may not know it, but we are both in that space.

I wanted to say goodbye, I say.

I'll be here for a while yet.

I may not be.

Where you going?

I hear the steelhead are running the best they've done in years.

You don't seem the type to torture fish.

I laugh. He's right.

Any excuse to stare at water moving over rocks.

He laughs, carefully. Watch out for bears.

The painkillers slip like winter into his blood. His eyelids droop. I say what I remember.

The heart is a white mountain
left of centre in the world.
The heart is dust. The heart is trees.
The heart is snowbound broken
rock in the locked ribs of a man
in the sun on the shore of the sea who is dreaming

sun on the snow, dreaming snow on the broken
rock, dreaming wind, dreaming winter.

My voice fades into the autumn twilight.
What else? he asks.
I thought he was asleep. It's hard to remember, I say.
He turns to look at me, waiting.

The heart is four hands serving soup
made of live meat and water.
The heart is a place. The heart is a name.

He waits.

My heart slips down the river, opens to the possibility of flooding. *Because even sorrow has a source*, I say. *For though it cannot fly, the heart is an excellent clamberer.*

Divining Isaac

When George Brampton hears what he did when his heart stopped, he laughs. He'd just emptied the dumpster behind Isadora's Bridal Boutique into the garbage truck and was beginning the complicated manoeuvre around the concrete posts the boutique's owner, Dora Rawlings, had poured when she bought her first Mercedes—posts to stop imbeciles like George from backing into her precious German steel.

The pain fell upon him like an axe blade. His left side clenched, drawing his foot clear off the clutch. His right foot slammed the gas pedal to the floor. The truck shot backward, knocked over a post, and cracked the brick firewall in the back of Dora's store. The post crumpled the left side of the silver Mercedes.

"I wish you could have seen Dora's face," Leonard says. Leonard Defoe owns the hardware store beside the boutique. "If it hadn't been for the miserable shape you're in, I'd have said it was worth it. I don't believe I've ever seen an unpunched face puff up like that."

George laughs through the oxygen nose clip, around the IV tubes and electrodes, and past the pain Leonard can see on his face. "Nobody hurt?"

"Nah. Dora's a little shook up and old Frank Evans's been heard to complain because the town went in the next day and pulled the posts right out."

Evans has been the town's driving tester for years. He likes to take sixteen-year-old girls down that stretch of alley so he can watch their bodies twist as they try to back around Dora's posts. Sixteen-year-old girls or anyone who shows up for the test in a car uncomfortably small for his three hundred pounds.

"Stop," George wheezes. "You're gonna kill me."

Silence, or the nearest thing to it, enters the intensive-care unit. The room doesn't get much use in this small-town hospital and has the cluttered look of a storage closet. The nurse sits off to one side, the green light of the heart monitor reflected in her pale face.

"What shape's the truck in?" George asks.

Leonard shifts in his chair. "Don't worry about the truck. Your family's out there chewing their fingernails. They sent me in to, well, talk to you. About things."

George rolls away and looks out the window at the mountain that blocks the town's afternoon sunlight all winter. The sun is behind it now, the deep descending blue sky opening itself to the stars. "Best view in the whole place."

"George."

"Go away, Leonard."

"George."

"Later."

Leonard looks down at the bright dome of his friend's bald head with its fringe of thick grey curls. He has never seen George without his Vern's Autobody cap, its bright yellow mesh misshapen from constant adjusting. Without the bulky lined coveralls, his small frame shrinks into frailty. Without the thick canvas gloves he wears to swing garbage bags, his hands, bruised from the IV needles, lie like brittle bones on the white sheet. Leonard squeezes George's shoulder. "Later."

Five heads swivel to look at Leonard when he steps into the noisy hospital corridor. George's four sons and his wife stand. Leonard takes off his glasses and rubs his eyes. "Don't do that," he says, backing away. The boys are all well over six feet and two hundred pounds; the mother isn't much smaller. Leonard is five feet eight inches. He shakes his head. "Later."

George isn't ready to talk about do-not-resuscitate orders and death, his family isn't ready to ask him, and Leonard is unwilling to admit that one of the few friends he has is going to die. Any time now.

He pauses beside the elevator, pulls a handful of feathers, beads, and wire from his pocket, and calls to George's wife. "I forgot this." He holds it out to her. "From Isaac." Her hand draws back, and Leonard has to jump to catch the bundle. "For Chrissake, woman, it's a present from his friend."

She turns away and moves toward the ICU. Leonard twists the beads over his fist and dodges past her. The nurse holds a finger to her lips. Leonard gives her the beads. "Make sure he gets these. They're from Isaac."

She nods and slips them into her pocket.

"Promise?"

She nods again.

There is only one smoker outside the hospital's main entrance. He keeps his distance from the bench where Isaac sits, hunched over, pushing trash around on the sidewalk with his foot: a couple of straws, cigarette butts, a Tim Hortons coffee cup, and an A&W burger bag. As Isaac stretches out a hand to twist a straw, the man grounds out his cigarette and wheels his IV stand right through whatever Isaac is arranging.

"Fuckin' stinks," he grumbles, and limps inside, the pale blue hospital housecoat straining across his bum.

The man is right. Isaac doesn't smell good. He looks bad too. Blond stubble sprouts from his pale skin. Leonard can see the reddened pores around his nose, the cracked lips. It is never a good idea to look too closely at Isaac.

"I gotta go, Isaac. You want a ride?"

Isaac bends over the garbage, jacket open. A wrench sticks out of one pocket. Ratty green mittens he never wears hang out the other. His red hands are chapped and cold-looking. He begins to rearrange the garbage.

"Okay. See you later."

Isaac won't step inside the hospital unless the ambulance or RCMP brings him, unconscious or cut up. But he will probably sit there until George comes out, which Leonard doesn't want to think about.

⁂

Isaac is as much a part of town as George's garbage truck. He rides an old three-speed bicycle with two big wicker panniers he stuffs full of the town's castoffs. He seems to have a deep rapport with bicycle parts: chains, wheels, sprockets. He fashions the metal into caricatures of people with sunburst sprocket faces, twisted metal spokes for hair, pedal cranks for flailing arms. Leonard has one mounted on the back wall of his store above the paints.

Kindhearted people tried to make Isaac wear a bicycle helmet. They stopped their efforts only when the Main Street merchants opened their doors one Monday morning and found, in the flower boxes that lined the street, a parade of familiarly dressed but headless, straw-stuffed bodies astride rusting bike frames, each with an old helmet stuffed up its ample ass.

"There's way more going on inside that boy's head than anyone imagines," Leonard said to George, who refused to cart the statues away.

George nodded. "He got the clothes perfect. That one's you to a tee."

"I know. When I saw it, first thing, I looked down to make sure I was dressed."

"Where'd he get them?"

"Out of some laundry I'd left in the back office. Easy pickings."

Then Leonard called the RCMP to say he'd personally pay any fines the boy incurred for not wearing a helmet, but he'd rather donate the money to the Cops for Cancer campaign. And he left the figure in the flower box until he saw a dog lift his leg to pee on what was really a perfectly good and quite expensive running shoe.

⁂

Leonard is still the new man on Main Street, but he and George somehow became friends. It started to happen, he thinks, the morning Granny Wing screeched at his back door, her stiff fingers scrabbling at his arm. She left food out behind the Alpine Noodle House for the town's few ratty street drunks. After they ate, she'd shoo them away with a huge wooden spatula. If she found one passed out in the dumpster, she'd throw the slippery restaurant garbage right on top of him. Or bang a big ladle on the side, the noise reverberating down the alley.

That morning Isaac was past rousing. Leonard called the ambulance. By the time the paramedics arrived to wrestle Isaac's bulky frame onto the stretcher, George had blocked the other end of the alley with his garbage truck.

"If people see him like this, they won't treat him as good," he muttered, scrunching his hat down tighter on his head.

Leonard had seen a bright welt across Isaac's cheek. "Not sure they treat him so hot now."

"Stupid son of a bitch gets himself into some godawful messes. Wish he'd stick to building stuff."

Leonard knew he wasn't the only one who picked up whichever of Isaac's creations he came across–the ones that could be moved. He liked the metal sculptures, but some were like the nightmares he'd had in the days when he drank too much. "The kid may be an artistic genius, but he's crazy as hell. Some of his stuff, boy, it's best to make it disappear before too many people see it."

George was mad. "The way this town treats him like a pet, like he's theirs somehow. To feed when they feel like it. To kick when they don't."

Leonard found himself curious to see what else George might say. He let his customers wait. "Guys like him, no matter where they live, they trigger meanness in some folks," he said. "Like his craziness draws out theirs."

"Do you think he'd be better off in one of those places where they'd take care of him?" George asked. "Clean him up? Give him stuff to work with?"

"Christ, no. Where do you think the crazies who get off on guys like Isaac find jobs? If you live wild like Isaac does, you need escape routes, not walls."

On the big post behind Leonard's cash register hangs a photograph full of brilliant yellow and splashes of red. People drawn to look closer find a dark man sitting against a temple wall, tangled, matted hair to his waist, a snake around his neck, and a devil's trident in his hand.

"A gentleman of the East in his retirement," Leonard will say if people ask. "He sells prayers. Me, in this hardware store, I sell the answers to your prayers."

"What'd you do before you moved here?" George asked him that spring morning as the ambulance backed out of the alley with Isaac.

"Don't ask, George. You take care of your garbage and I'll take care of mine."

George pushed his hat back on his head and spat gently at Leonard's feet. "I take care of everybody's garbage, Leonard. Mine, yours, even Isaac's. Hospital visiting hours start at two. I'll check on him then. Granny Wing will be worried sick." He swung up into his truck. "You go up after supper. Try to make sure they keep him in overnight. Clean him up and feed him."

"I hate hospitals, George."

"Christ almighty, who doesn't?"

George and Leonard were in their late fifties, feeling slow and stiff in the night when they had to get up, dozing as they waited for their reluctant piss to be released. But otherwise still strong, able to ignore the thinning, greying hair, the thickening knuckles, not seeing the lines they shaved over every day.

Isaac was still young, but somehow damaged. He never spoke, though he understood language. You had to watch his eyes to see what he wanted. His eyes moved over the surfaces of things like nervous fingers.

When Leonard locked up his store that afternoon, he was surprised to find himself walking up the hill to the hospital. And he felt as if he'd failed somehow when they told him Isaac had been released. But even if Isaac did wake up in a warm bed, he'd never stretch, luxuriating in his youth and strength, Leonard thought as he wandered through the evening sounds of the town's residential streets. The boy was scared deep inside. He never walked down a sidewalk simply enjoying the unexpected wonder of the world. Even when he was discovered busy at making something, he would look up startled, like a stray dog expecting to be hit.

Leonard had never before thought of looking for Isaac. He pretty much had the run of the hardware store. He'd borrow a blowtorch, pick up solder, wire, spray paint. So he showed up often enough to keep Leonard from getting around to wondering where he might be.

In that mild spring evening, through a town released from winter's darkness, Leonard wandered, adrift in neighbourhoods he'd never paid attention to. Stepping around puddles in flooding alleys, he calculated the tilt on sagging garages, heard tattered plastic flapping at the windows of garden sheds at the bottom of people's yards. These were the places where Isaac might find shelter.

"Did you take him home?" Leonard asked George the next morning.

George laughed and folded the beak of his hat right back, scratching under the band. "The wife would kill me if I brought Isaac into the house. It's hard enough for me to get inside, what with garbage and germs. I've gotta drop my coveralls on the porch and walk to the shower in my shorts. She does a damn good job of keeping me and the boys in line." His smile was like sunshine. "Not that we let her overdo it."

It's like those movies his mother once cried over, Leonard thinks now. The happy family kind. George's boys always track him down when they get in from the bush, idling pickup and garbage truck elbow to elbow, talking. The wife sews him special upholstered cushions for his truck. He's rigged up carriers on each side so he can hold on to stuff he knows someone needs. When people come home from work, they find garden tools, lawn furniture, tire rims they might have mentioned a month before. And he saves junk for Isaac.

⁂

Isaac's present hangs from the IV stand: brilliant blue electrical cord stripped down to the copper every quarter of an inch to look like blue and copper beads; another strand of washers–from his store, Leonard figures–separated by what could only be sequins from Isadora's Bridal Boutique; a third strand of dark shrivelled berries and dangling cedar waxwing tail and wing feathers, the thick waxy drops of red and yellow catching the afternoon light.

"My heart's had it," George says. Leonard can hear bubbling in his chest. "My lungs are filling up."

"Shit." Leonard looks out the window, at the sun emerging from the west side of the peak. "Are you ready for this?"

"Don't have much choice. This is one corner I can't back out of. The only way's straight ahead into another fucking fire wall. Is that what you'd call ready?" One hand lifts off the bed and points behind Leonard. "Even Dora got me flowers. She must be planning the party already. Good riddance to bad rubbish."

"So what do you want us to do with you, buddy? Your boys want to do what's right." Leonard tries to laugh. "How they got so fond of you I can't figure. I never found your company that pleasant."

"The wife never wanted me to be a garbageman. She wanted me to try to get on the road crew or work in the yard. But I like it."

"Somebody famous wrote a book about a garbageman."

George nods.

"You read it?"

"Nah."

"Me neither. But I heard he had bagpipes at his funeral."

George's hand twitches. Leonard takes it in his. The flesh has caved in beneath the calluses. "Don't let young Stanley get his hands on me, Leonard. I don't want that bastard touching me."

The local funeral home has a garden that George has always found unseemly. Luscious peonies, scarlet runners, and the biggest tomatoes in town.

"I don't want bits of me ending up in his garden."

"You wanna be buried in the dump?"

"Christ, no. That's the very stew of hell down under that ground." George squeezes Leonard's hand with surprising strength. "Crisp me up good. Get the boys to put me in a box and take me straight to the cooker. Be done with it."

"You want your ashes spread on the dump?

"Fuck off."

"Your family's breathing down my neck pretty hard. And my neck's getting stiff looking up at all of them."

George starts to laugh, but it turns into a bubbling cough. The nurse comes over and hefts him into a sitting position, holding an arm across his stomach to help him. Leonard looks away. When it's finished, she tidies him up and draws Leonard aside. He smells the soap on her hands, the shampoo in her hair as she tells him she is going to call the family. That there isn't much more time.

When the door closes behind her, Leonard is scared. George is grey and breathing in short gasps. "Hang in there, buddy. Your boys'll be here soon."

"Christ, Leonard, I'm scared."

"Me too. You better wait for them, you bugger, or they'll kill me. Don't you dare stop breathing now."

"Serve you right."

Leonard leans back, tries to relax. "You know, when I was a kid, I always envied garbagemen. They seemed like they were cutting school and whooping it up. Three, four of them on a truck, riding the sides like you weren't supposed to. You've had good fun out of it, George."

George's breathing slows into something more peaceful. "I ain't going yet. Tell me about Isaac."

"Isaac is still stinking up the smokers' bench out front. He hasn't moved as far as anyone can see, though I suspect he disappears for a couple of hours to sleep somewhere and take a leak. The cook's feeding him."

"Silly bugger."

"Who's his kin?"

"It's an ugly story, Leonard. You don't wanna know details."

"Catholic?"

"None of your business. Why?"

Leonard pulls out another gift: two bright yellow straws tied into a cross, a cardboard coffee cup pummelled and twisted into the shape of a man stuck to the cross with gooseberry thorns.

"Jesus," George murmurs.

"You got your rosary up there, now a crucifix. What comes next?"

"Beats me. I don't go to church."

"Want me to tie it here?"

"The old lady'll have a fit if she sees it. Put it in the drawer there."

"That boy is suffering."

"He won't come in?"

Leonard shakes his head. "He'll meet you outside."

George twists restlessly. "Outside, up there, down below, who cares? It won't be these eyes he'll be looking into. You ever notice his eyes? They're always sliding over things, snagging on something he wants, sliding away, then coming back like he's running his big ugly hands over it."

"I try not to think of all the things he's seen."

"I talked to the doctor this morning, Leonard. Told her to let me go. None of those jumper cables."

"Well..."

"I should have died there that day in the alley. In my truck."

"It's kind of you to give us a bit of time, old buddy."

George rolls away, looks out the window at the bright snow on the mountain. "I remember the first time I took notice of Isaac. They must have kicked him out of whatever house or school he was in because he showed up on the streets. I found him passed out under the dumpster behind Dora's. He was lying on his back–his hair was longer then–and he, or somebody, had tied it full of tiny twists of cloth and ribbon. Dozens of them. He had a red satin band around his neck, bits of bright cloth scattered over his clothes."

Leonard unhooks the rosary from the IV stand, slides his fingers over the wire, strokes the feathers.

"That white stuff brides wear was coming out from behind his shoulders. Looked like wings. The red band looked like blood. I thought at first it was a girl with her throat slit. I was bending over her when I saw the whiskers and smelled the booze and piss. But his eyes opened, I guess, before the disgust I felt showed on my face."

Leonard leans in closer to catch his words. The pale skin of George's back shows through the gap in the hospital gown.

"He just lay there looking at me. It shook me up. I didn't want anyone to see him like that. So I started untying the little ribbons. But that was gonna take days, so I got out my knife and he looked scared then. Like he'd had business with knives before. But he didn't move. He looked at me and I cut off most of his hair. I was scared too. I knew if someone saw us like that it would turn ugly. When I was done and helped him up, I saw this big ragged boy looked like he should be milking cows and this pile of bright cloth and twists of bright hair and ribbon scattered in the dirt. I wasn't sure I'd done the right thing." George turns finally and looks at Leonard, tries to see what's in the eyes of his friend.

Leonard folds the beads into George's hands. "You did okay."

"Like he was on his way somewhere and got stuck here. Never got finished." George's eyes fill. His breath comes faster and shallower.

Leonard bends closer.

"Keep an eye out for him."

"I will. I am."

The door opens and the room fills with Bramptons.

⸙

The next morning Leonard slumps beside Isaac on the bench and tells him George is gone. Leonard isn't sure he understands. "Like the cedar waxwing," he says. "Dead."

Two of the Brampton sons drive up. "We need your help,

Mr. Defoe."

He doesn't move.

"The house is full of those Women's Institute ladies talking about doing it proper with the undertaker."

Leonard stirs. The nearest boy holds up his hand. "Don't worry. We know what Dad wants. I got the box right here."

"Isaac's gotta see him, or he'll never leave this bench."

The boys look at each other and don't look at Isaac who isn't looking at any of them. "Ah, sure, we don't mind old Isaac."

Leonard and Isaac hop into the back of the pickup with the coffin, a plain box of pale birch planks, and ride around to the back door of the hospital. When the boys lift it off, Isaac takes the coffin lid in his arms. Leonard's eyes blur when he sees the grey wool blanket and the pillow with its clean white case. He remembers the weight of a dog, wrapped in a similar blanket, heavy in his arms. His reluctance to release it to the cold soil. He is glad George is going to be cremated.

The boys lift the box onto their shoulders, and Leonard opens the back doors where a nurse waits with a stretcher. They wheel the coffin down the hallway into the morgue. In one wall there are four metal squares with handles. The nurse pulls out a long drawer, and one boy sucks in his breath when he sees the long white plastic bag. "He's in that?"

The nurse looks at Leonard and nods.

"Good Christ, it's like we're taking him to the dump." Same boy.

"What's he wearing?" the other boy asks.

The nurse whispers to Leonard, "Nothing."

Leonard feels his balls contract and goose bumps rise on his shoulders at the thought of George's cold bare skin resting against that plastic. One of the boys is retching into the corner sink. Leonard whispers to the nurse. She nods and skitters out the door.

The three men stand in the cold silence, trying not to inhale, none of them able to touch one another for comfort. Or to touch George.

The nurse comes back in with a package. She empties out George's coveralls, their dark blue silvered with dust. "Wait outside," she says. "I'll get him ready."

One of the boys moves to help.

"Go on," she says. "You don't need to do this. It'll only take a minute."

A little later the boys go back in to lift George into the box. As they lay him gently down, the air, pressed out of the feathers in the pillow, puffs through his curls. Leonard is glad he doesn't have to feel the cold weight of his friend's body in his arms. He suddenly wishes there was a warm body waiting somewhere to hold him.

"Christ almighty, Dad." One of the boys sobs and turns away, his face crumpled.

The other one wipes his nose on his sleeve. "Let's get going. We've got a long drive."

They wheel George out into the bright February sunlight. Isaac is still sitting on the wheel well in the back of the pickup. The boys slide the coffin beside him and wait. He looks at George's face, whiskers poking through the blue skin, the fringe of curls lifting slightly in the open air. He reaches out to touch the shining bald circle, then pulls from his pocket a filthy yellow cap and fits it on George's head. Vern's Autobody. The boys whoop and slap him on the back. "Son of a bitch! Good man, Isaac."

Isaac watches as the boys fit the lid onto the box. The older one pulls a small electric screwdriver from his pocket. The other hands him the screws one at a time.

"Come on out," Leonard says. "These boys have to go. Maybe Granny Wing will give us some lunch."

Isaac stares past his right ear.

"Come on, Isaac," one boy says.

Isaac puts his hand on the pale wood and hunkers back against the cab's rear window.

"We're going all the way to the city, Isaac. You'll freeze." The boy's sorrow is turning to anger.

Isaac doesn't move.

Leonard reaches in behind the seat and tosses Isaac a greasy sleeping bag. "Away you go. Isaac'll make sure he doesn't slide around too much."

The pause is barely noticeable. One of the boys hands Isaac his screwdriver. "Keep an eye on those screws. Don't want them coming loose."

Leonard slams the tailgate shut. He slaps the side of the truck as they drive off toward the mountains in the east. The sun reflects off the back window of the cab, and Leonard sees the brightness shining in Isaac's hair as he sits, one hand on the box, holding George steady.

Disappearance

Evy Dumont, thirteen and thin as a chicken, drains a glass of orange juice and climbs out the window of her second-floor apartment to eat her cold breakfast pizza on the tiny balcony overlooking Main Street. She shivers even though the morning sun has been shining on the balcony for a couple of hours already. It doesn't matter that it's June 21. Even the longest day of the year in this northern town starts out cold. And because it's a Sunday, empty.

She looks over the hardware store across the street, over the tops of the scrubby little houses in the low part of town, over the highway, and up eight thousand feet to the snowcapped mountain. It's the only thing that makes the town different from any other gritty northern highway gas stop, a difference the town councillors never fail to emphasize.

Her dad pokes fun at them for their smugness. "You'd think they put it there," he says about the mountain. "Had it shipped over from the Alps, then made everyone put up flowered shutters and peaked roofs so European tourists would feel right at home."

Coming from the prairies, Yves Dumont resists the mountains. Evy wants to go up there. She wants to see farther than the view from the second floor. She yawns. The day's first mosquito floats onto the balcony and circles her bare ankles. She scratches one foot with the other and squints down into the shadow cast by the hardware store. Leonard Cant Defoe waves and climbs the ladder to his roof. He's been watching for her.

Cant Hardware, an old wood-frame building that stands out in all the early photographs of the town, stark and solid in a wasteland of stumps, tents, and mud, predates the town planners. Twelfth Avenue runs smack into its front door, stops for a block, and then takes up again to continue down to the highway. Every couple of years an exuberant driver lands in the window display.

Since January, the window has been empty. The store looks derelict. But that's about to change. Last night Defoe was out on his roof, installing a complicated system of hooks, pulleys, and rolls of canvas. Evy spotted him when she stomped into the living room to sulk, escaping her dad's anger. "Hey, Mr. Defoe," she yelled across to him, "what are you doing?"

"If you can hold on until morning, you just might see, girlie."

"Are you finished, Mr. Defoe? Finished your great idea?"

"I think I might be."

Evy remembered the day Defoe had his great idea. He'd had a rough winter. Sometime after the Christmas shopping frenzy, his girlfriend, who managed the shoe store across the street, had flounced into his store, screamed insults at him, and shortly afterward left town. Nobody knew what had ended their volatile affair, and no one had the courage to ask. He barely spoke to his customers, grumbled over the trouble it was to take their money. He emptied the warehouse, piling all his stock into the store. He backed shelves right up to the windows and stuffed them with dusty gadgets no one could remember a use for. Instead of brightening with the lengthening days, the store grew dim. The occasional shaft of afternoon sunlight shining through the open door increased the gloom, illuminating dust motes spiralling like silt in the river. The air felt thick, old. But, in spite of Defoe, customers found themselves lingering, wistful, in the musty quiet.

Evy, who used his store like a backyard, was worried. She'd overhear people saying they should do something about the mess, that Defoe was a disgrace, the store a health risk. She tried jokes, but he'd turn his back. Then Jackie Fredericks came in to buy the salt he'd pour an inch thick on the sidewalk in front of his toy store so no one could sue him if they slipped.

"Fredericks is a complicated fellow," Defoe had explained to her. "He hates to part with his money, but feels bad making kids part with theirs. So they sucker him by counting out their pennies one at a time, never having quite enough. And he knows it."

Evy walked up behind Defoe, looked at Fredericks, and put one finger to her lips while she lifted a hair dryer off the counter at Defoe's back and tucked it under her sweatshirt as if she were going to steal it. Fredericks's face opened up into a beautiful grin as he looked right through Defoe at Evy. Disgusted at the man's lack of subtlety, Evy waited for Defoe to bark at her. Instead, he stared back at Fredericks for several awkward seconds.

"That smile is a wonder, Jackie." His voice was soft. The man blushed, stammered, and fumbled in his pockets for the right change. "I wish it was for my benefit, but I figure those days are passed. There is, however, a certain reward to be gained from simply being in its path." Evy put the hair dryer back on the counter. When he started talking like that, she never knew what was going to happen.

He waved Fredericks out the door. "You've given me a great idea." He refused the money. "Ideas are valuable, Jackie. This one's worth at least a bag of salt."

He watched Fredericks scuttle away, then, without turning, said, "Having you behind the till instead of haunting the aisles might be good for business. Scoot up on this stool and I'll show you how to work the cash register."

She caught on quickly and didn't think anything more about the "great idea" until she realized Defoe was leaving her more and more to mind the store while he disappeared into his warehouse across the alley. He ignored her questions. She didn't mind, really, because at least he'd stopped snapping at everybody. And she found she liked showing off to customers; she could find casing nails blindfolded and knew exactly where Defoe hid the discounted potting soil. She protested when he gave her a pay cheque.

"If you don't want it, give it away," he said. "Give it to the winos so they can buy booze instead of solvents. Or save it so you can buy me out before this place drives me crazy."

❧

Evy's earliest memories are of standing on a stool and looking out the apartment window down across the street to the hardware store, the splintered wood of the windowsill fragrant with the dampness of her tears. She'd walked past the store on her way home from school since fourth grade when she told her father she would no longer wait for him in the noise and squabbling at the babysitter's. But she hadn't much liked the store at first. The Bennings, who had owned it since the grandfather built it in 1913, filled the air with cigarette smoke and gossip. Whenever she walked through the doors, she felt their appraising glances. She had keen instincts and knew she and her dad were somehow suspect.

All that had changed when Defoe bought the store. He'd come to town a few years before, run a couple of businesses along the frontage road where no one much cared about the niceties of window displays, lost a wife somewhere along the way. Moving into a piece of history right on Main Street, well, that caught everyone's attention. Her dad, ever scornful of the town's pretensions, had laughed over the things he heard as he went from business to business cleaning and repairing photocopiers, fax machines, and cash registers.

Yelling down from the balcony on a busy Friday evening, he'd congratulated Defoe and said he hoped he wasn't going to put up any of those goddamned flowered shutters. Evy had drawn her head back from the window like a frightened turtle, but smiled when she heard the answering laugh.

A few days later she'd been loitering at the crosswalk when Defoe called her over. A ladder leaned against his roof. "Will you hold this for me?"

Evy looked at him. A medium-size man, with thinning red hair, blue shirt, blue jeans, and running shoes. Older than her dad. He waited. "Sure, I guess."

She watched him stretch to tighten the screws on his new sign: CANT HARDWARE. "Doesn't that need an apostrophe?" she asked. Back then she'd just started grade five and had learned about apostrophes that morning at school. He laughed so hard, she was afraid. "Stop it or I'll let go. You're going to fall and flatten me."

He came down the ladder and stretched out one of the biggest hands she'd ever seen. Fingers like the beef sausages her dad liked to barbecue. "Leonard Cant Defoe," he'd said as she stared. He wiggled his fingers.

She held out her hand and watched it disappear. "Evy Dumont. As in Chevy."

Her dad had laughed when she told him. And told her to be careful. "Can't trust anyone," he'd said.

But Evy knew she could trust Defoe. When she went into his store, she sniffed and asked him, "Where are the animals?"

"Sorry, kid, they're gone. Can't abide cages and fish tanks."

She sniffed again. "Me neither."

⁂

Evy wants a dog. A little dog with wiry hair to wriggle on her lap on sunny summer mornings. To share her pizza. She licks her fingers. She wants something to do with her restless hands, her restless body. She is waiting to finish her last week of grade seven, of elementary school; she is waiting for her period to begin; she is waiting for high school, lockers, and crowded hallways, the intoxicating sight of older boys. She is waiting to begin her summer holidays, to see all her prairie cousins and her great-grandma, to swim in the South Saskatchewan River. She is waiting to see Defoe's great idea.

He prowls across his roof, sun illuminating his thin hair, his shirt already damp from exertion. He is checking every rope and pulley. Nervous, Evy yawns. She can't imagine anything that could live up to the town's expectations. Or her own. She hopes whatever he's got on that canvas doesn't get him arrested as he almost was last month for threatening the men who invited him into the room at the back of Eddie's Fine Furnishings, fed him rye, and suggested he do something about his dirty windows and messy store.

Defoe never really got the hang of window displays. Not like the bookstore with its Gypsy bangles and dangling angels, not like the clothing stores with their autumn leaves strewn artfully across rugged jackets or satin wedding dresses, not like the bakery with its seasonal action pieces: electric trains circling green-icing hay fields and frosted mountain cakes, Santa riding a gingerbread sleigh and waving.

Most likely that alone wouldn't have mattered, but he also refused to join any of the men's service clubs. They'd all asked him because a hardware store owner comes in handy when it's time to put new grass seed on the ball diamonds or new paint on the playground fences.

Evy's dad knew about the threats because when Defoe threw his glass at Eddie's head, it bounced off and emptied into the photocopier, and he'd had to go fix the damage.

"To think I'm drinking rye with the likes of you bastards!" Defoe had yelled. "Rye, for God's sake. My old mother was right. This shit's only fit for drowning snakes."

"I don't understand him," Eddie told Yves Dumont. "It was the best Crown Royal."

Dumont hadn't drunk a drop of hard liquor since the day he got a phone call from one of his wilder girlfriends, saying she was going to jail and had this kid who was his. Didn't want social workers getting her. Name's Evy, she'd said. After you. He sympathized with Defoe. Except for Evy, rye had never brought him anything but misery. So Dumont had talked Eddie out of pressing charges. Told him to give Defoe a bit more time. He had something cooking, he'd said.

Evy thought it was all silly until Eddie's friends came around and told Defoe whatever he was planning for the front of his building, he'd need a building permit. "Get the fuck outta here," he'd yelled, emptying the store of everyone but old Mrs. Rochester, who hadn't heard a thing in twenty years and stole a five-pound bag of bird seed every Friday, and Evy who was behind the till.

Evy curled her lip. "Mr. Defoe," she began.

"You!" he'd yelled. "You get outta here too. Probably the one blabbed to them in the first place, you little sneak."

She jumped off the stool, hands on hips. "Me? How could I tell them anything? I don't know any more than anyone else, even though until now I was probably the only friend you had left." She was almost crying. "And it's no fair calling me a sneak!"

At this point Mrs. Rochester shuffled by them on her way out the door, the bird seed bulging out of her huge purse. They both held their breath and nodded politely to her. Evy's heart pounded in fury and sudden fear. Fear that she had said too much as she watched Defoe's blood rise into his face. Fear that he was going to explode, taking his store and her along with him.

Instead, he opened the door for Mrs. Rochester and walked out behind her. For one horrible moment, Evy thought he was going to confront the old woman, but he turned the other way and disappeared.

⁂

Evy hears her dad moving around behind her in the apartment. She crushes a mosquito probing among the fine hairs of her forearm and flicks the corpse off her finger. She stands, stretches, and calls across the street. "How much longer, Mr. Defoe? The bugs have found me."

"Ten minutes. Get your old man."

"Right." Evy climbs back inside, blind in the sudden dimness. She wishes her dad was an old man, not some cute guy women flirt with. She feels a sudden ache sweep through her because he's started to respond. In the kitchen at the back of the apartment, he crosses back and forth between the stove and the fridge. She doesn't want to share this place with anyone but him. And, occasionally, Defoe.

⋙

The first time he came up was right after he'd given the salt to Jackie Fredericks. Standing in a watery streak of afternoon light, he said, "I'll need to get up there," and pointed to her balcony. She hesitated. Nothing she'd seen had changed that safe feeling she felt the first time she'd walked into his newly claimed store and saw the caged animals gone, the gossip stopped, and Defoe standing behind the tall counter, largely indifferent to his customers and stock.

From those first days, he'd let Evy, who had a deep need to hide, sit on the bottom shelf under the counter where customers couldn't see her. Tracing the dusty wires coiled into electric outlets, she'd inhale the smell of running shoes and WD 40 and listen to the conversations. She'd watch his leather running shoes, rolled slightly sideways like the boots on a man who rode horses, move in neat steps as he punched in prices, packed bags, got the door for a burdened customer.

When things were quiet, he'd talk to her, not caring if it looked as if he was speaking to himself. He told her he didn't know what had possessed him to get into the hardware business in the first place. "People come in here when they have a problem–ants to poison, a mouse to trap, a plugged toilet, broken dishes, a burnt-out kettle."

She'd join in. "A lost key, a broken lock."

"Cat shit, frozen gas line, burst water pipes."

They'd continue until one repeated something or a customer came in.

"It's not like a bookstore or a clothing store or even a damned shoe store where people go to amuse or decorate themselves." He'd stare around his dusty domain. "It's a place of broken things."

"Sort of like a hospital."

"Only worse. Once you leave a hospital you're either getting better or you've died. The folks who leave here are going to have to stick their heads under a sink, down a well, or into a car engine, or worse yet, climb a ladder, breathe in sawdust, paint fumes."

When she got bored there, she'd wander the store and play with dishes, sort nails, open boxes of lawn seed and sift the smooth contents through her fingers. Sometimes she'd unstack a shelf of kitty-litter bags, climb in, then pull the bags back in behind her. Or the sisal door mats. They had come a long way, she'd think, from somewhere hot and dusty. They'd prickle through the thin cotton of her T-shirt the way her dad's whiskers did on Sunday morning after he went all day Saturday without shaving. If she woke him up too early, he'd chase her around the apartment, scraping her cheeks and neck with his whiskers.

The comfort of hiding was so intense, one day she'd fallen asleep. When Defoe bent into the darkness behind the dog-food bags and shook her awake, she'd struggled to surface from great depths.

"How did you find me?" she'd asked as she stumbled out, hair mussed, clothes filthy. She'd always thought it was her secret.

"Do you think I don't keep track of my customers, girlie, even if they never buy a damn blasted thing?"

Her irritation had dissolved when she saw her father sitting on the cat food stacked at the end of the aisle. Sorrow, terror, relief, and fury had crumpled his face. "Hey, what's the panic?"

"Leave him alone. He was thinking the worst after Eddie told him you were likely over here where you've been seen hanging around a lot lately." Defoe's voice tightened. "He was ready to punch me out when he came through that door." He piled the dog food back on the shelf. Evy hesitated, appalled by her father's sudden helplessness.

⁂

When Evy came to live with her father, she wouldn't talk at first. He could see she was afraid of him. Clutching the small rock she'd kept in her fist since they left Saskatchewan, she had paced out the edges of his new apartment on her three-year-old legs. He'd unpacked her few boxes while she watched from the door. He went into the kitchen to escape her frightened stare, wondering what he would have to do to make her trust him. He made grilled-cheese sandwiches.

In spite of his grandmother's insistence, he didn't know if he could do this. He hadn't believed at first that Evy was even his. His grandmother had sniffed the toddler's arms and belly, rubbed her hair between her fingers, then blown into the terrified face to see the way she wrinkled her nose. "She's yours, all right. Takes after your mother, God help you both," she'd said. "Have to get yourself a town job now. Can't be in the bush all week and raise a kid."

The apartment that day seemed more silent than any four walls he'd lived between. He'd set out the sandwiches, ketchup, and milk on the small table and gone to get the girl. She had disappeared. The terror he'd felt during the frantic search, and the lurching relief he'd experienced when he found her asleep under a cardboard box, had confirmed for him his fatherhood.

Watching the strands of black hair lift and settle across her thin cheek as she breathed, he'd tried to imagine what had made her hide. Then, when he figured it out, at least in part, he had tried to turn off his imagination because it made him want to visit his ex-girlfriend in the prison back east and throttle her. As for Evy, well, he had promised himself she wouldn't see anything that would make her want to hide again.

As they'd settled in to get to know each other, he'd hoped her need to hide was going, that he could abandon his daily terror over the possibility of losing her. But when he looked down the aisle of the hardware store at her smudged and anxious face, he knew he would never lose his fear and nor would she.

⁂

Evy had sidled up to Dumont, pulled off his hat, and messed up his hair. He upended her across his knees. Defoe moved as if to interfere, but stopped when he saw Dumont's fingers walk up her spine. "No disappearing," he said, emphasizing each syllable with a jab of his fingers. "You promised."

She wriggled out of his grasp, straddled his knees, and held his face between her hands. "I was just playing. Pretending I had a dog. I mean, what's the big deal? I mostly always get home before you do."

Defoe hissed. "So you've been coming in here all this time and never told your dad?"

He squatted, his face so close she could smell his gum. Evy squirmed, but her dad held her.

"You–" Defoe swallowed his curses "–idiot. Anything could have happened, and where would that have left us? Me in jail probably and your dad in the loony bin and some creep out there laughing."

Dumont looked at Defoe, trying to explain what looked like neglect. "I thought we had a system. I send her faxes from my jobs and when she gets home from school, she sends me one saying she's okay."

"She snookered us both," Defoe said, still rattled. "Get outta here now. I have to balance the till before morning, so I need a good head start. And don't come back in here without your dad's say-so. Hiding and sneaking are two different things."

⁂

With both sides of Main Street covered, Evy had never felt safer in her life. So when Defoe asked to go up to the apartment, her hesitation was imperceptible and had more to do with trying to remember whether her underpants might be hanging from any doorknobs.

He turned the sign on his door to CLOSED, and she took him through the narrow alley between the shoe and furniture stores. He hesitated and put one hand against the wall of the shoe store as if to warm it. She looked away until she heard him sigh, then they climbed the stairs. To dispel his gloom, she chattered as she showed him the apartment. The strip of linoleum just inside the door served as a mudroom. The kitchen table where she and her dad sat for breakfast had a great view of the mountain. The little doorway in the back corner went into a tiny bathroom with a half-size bathtub and snaky shower hose.

She described all this to him and said she really liked it because she could watch what was going on but feel safe and hidden, right out there in the open. "And I can keep an eye on things for you."

He looked out the window and held up his thumb as if he was measuring something. Then he started sketching in a little notebook he'd pulled out of his jacket. He turned away when she tried to look. Pouting, she wandered around, dropping her jacket, pack, hat. Defoe ignored her until the fax machine beeped. He watched Evy gather up the pages already scrolled out onto the worn hardwood floor around the machine. She sorted them as the latest page slithered out.

"He started off his day in Zellers. Someone dumped coffee into the photocopier. Then he drove out to the airport and fixed their fax, then he went to do the regular cleaning for the high school, and then, look, he was at my school too. I missed him." She read the last one. "He's finished at the glass factory and will pick up a chicken grill from A&W for supper."

"Did you send him one?"

"I did." She came pretty close to flouncing and threw the faxes in a pile on the old maroon couch. "What are you going to do?" She nodded at his notebook.

"If you could look out that window and see anything in the world that you wanted, anything at all, what would it be?"

She looked. The battered old building, its layers of renovations as saggy as her great-grandma's old brassiere. The old church. The empty parking lot. "I'd have to think about that."

"So think."

She pulled her hair back into a ponytail, twirled it a couple of times, and let it go. "If I'm really bored, I like to watch the trucks roar up and down on Friday nights. Sometimes, late, I see kids I know in the shadows. I'm scared I'll see them do something stupid and they'll see me. But I like to watch." She shivered and hugged herself with thin arms. "Sunday mornings I see these girls all dressed up, walking to church. I mean, no one ever dresses like that for anything else. Dressed up but ugly."

"Okay, okay. That's what you see. But what would you like to see?"

She crossed her arms and slouched against the window frame. "Whatever. You sound like my art teacher." Her voice turned plummy, British, her eyes closed. "'Imagine, boys and girls. Imagine yourselves in the deepest jungle. Now open your eyes and look around. What do you see?'" Her eyes opened. "I open my eyes and see Jason Malachuck's dirty T-shirt right in front of me, I see the black splotch on the floor beside my desk that's been there all year, and I see grey snow out the window. So that's what I draw." Her voice dropped to a giggle. "And does that ever piss Mrs. Moberly right off."

"Say the store wasn't there. What would you put in its place?"

"Jeez. Talk about a pain. You don't give up easy, do you?"

He waited.

She put her finger against her nose, then pulled on it. "Okay, okay. It's hard to imagine what isn't there. Especially when something else is there. Like, you know, when they built the new liquor store? I walked through that empty lot for a whole year. Grade four. All year. Now I can't remember what it looked like without the liquor store. Not at all. As soon as you put something up like that, it's like it's always been there. Whatever went before disappears."

Defoe was no longer paying attention.

"Like when you moved your counter. The first week I kept running right into it, and now I can't remember where it was before."

Defoe's lips tightened and his pencil stopped. Evy realized she'd made a mistake. Defoe's anger could flare unexpectedly. Especially when anyone reminded him of his foolishness. The woman in the shoe store. The store beneath their feet.

She was somebody's sister-in-law: coffee-coloured skin, bright lipstick, exotic. She'd been in the hardware store a couple of times, asking Defoe for advice. Evy didn't get it at first, but she sensed something happening. The store's air currents felt turbulent. Defoe was overwrought–kind but edgy.

The first clue was his window display. They'd always been off-kilter. Hunting gear in spring, fly rods when all the rivers were frozen, lawn mowers in January. But that February he'd filled the window with electric heaters, generators, candles, propane torches, kerosene lanterns, flashlights, and about thirty lamps. He'd lined the backdrop with aluminum foil, then left the lights burning all night. Evy and her dad looked at it as if it was one of those puzzles in kids' magazines: "What do these objects have in common?"

Then, on February 14, the winter shoes were gone from the shoe-store window across the street. Mannequin toes peeked out of stiletto-heeled sandals into a sea of pink Styrofoam chips that curled like licking tongues. Mannequin feet were kicked up, and one mannequin leg wore a black stocking held up by a garter belt. When Evy brought her dad down to see, he looked back and forth across the street and laughed out loud.

"He is hot and so is she," he chortled. "This feels like July, not February." He was laughing so hard he could barely stand up. He started singing, "Hunka hunka burning love," until Evy dragged him back upstairs away from the stares of passing shoppers.

The woman's sister-in-law got the garter belt out of the window pretty quickly, and a few sensible shoes reappeared. But not soon enough. Word filtered out. Defoe seemed oblivious to the nudges and winks. People could have robbed him blind, emptied his whole store out the back door while he gazed across the street at the delectable pink of those Styrofoam tongues. In the evenings he massaged the crick in his neck. That was when he'd moved the counter–so he could look out his front door across the street to her store.

Evy and all of Main Street watched the relationship evolve over the next year. Evy mostly uncomprehending, but sensing a violence to it that made her want to hide again. When things were good, Defoe made his customers nervous with his bright eyes and determination to help. When they were fighting, Defoe let the light bulbs burn out in his window, allowed dust to accumulate. He didn't shave or answer questions. He'd point and grunt.

The girlfriend was more extreme. She'd empty the window of everything except one shoe, its spike heel embedded in a mannequin's thigh, or pinning a foot to the ground. Her friends from the clothing store next door would go in and talk her into removing the injured body parts, put her on the plane for a weekend in Vancouver, and send in their daughters to set up a display more suitable for family viewing.

Sulking, Evy swore she could smell the woman's strong perfume drifting up into their apartment. She made gagging noises. Her dad tried to explain why people get so heated up, why some of her classmates were going gaga over boys, giggling and smirking. "It's not all bad," he told her. "If I hadn't lost my marbles over a woman, you wouldn't be here." He tried to divert Evy, encouraged her to have friends over, to stop worrying. "Defoe, after all," he said, "is getting lucky. It's worth a little scorching."

Evy heard the longing in her father's voice and watched him finding it harder and harder not to look. His eyes straying to women's legs, breasts. She tried not to care, but felt herself falling, disappearing, whenever his attention strayed. It got worse when he started to tease her about boys. In not very many months, he told her, boys would be looking at her and thinking the way boys think.

⋙

"We need a break," Dumont says when he joins Evy on the balcony to watch Defoe's progress. "We need a visit with Grandma to straighten us out." His mouth is full of waffle.

Evy doesn't answer. She is still a little mad at him. The night before, a fax arrived from the school librarian. "Found this fax left in memory. How sweet. You're a lucky girl, Evy." Dumont had been in a hurry and hadn't waited to make sure his last fax home on Friday night had gone through. It had been silly–about picking up his favourite girl and going out on the town.

Evy snatched the fax from him. Her voice shrilled as she read the rest. "'I'm having a little party next week. Why don't you two come on over?' And, oh, there's a cute little map with perfect teacher printing. Aren't we honoured?"

"Evy! She's trying to be nice."

"She's got the hots for you. I've watched her." She stuck a finger down her throat. "Barf! There's no way I'm setting foot in her house."

"For Chrisssakes, your mind is as dirty as your mother's!"

In the silence a deep well opened between them. He slumped over the kitchen table, hands covering his face. She encased her thirteen-year-old heart in bitterness and stomped down the hall to sulk in the living room. To see Defoe on his roof was a gift. "Come on up!" she yelled. "We're just going to make popcorn."

She went back to the kitchen, slammed cupboard doors, tossed a bag into the microwave. "Pull yourself together, Daddy," she sneered when they heard Defoe's footsteps cross the porch.

"Sounds a mite crackly in here," Defoe said from the open door. "You sure you want company?"

Dumont rolled his eyes. "You might not want it, but I'd say we need it." He nodded toward Evy, one hip against the counter, arms crossed, waiting for the corn to finish popping.

Defoe ran his fingers through his hair. "Figure I can handle it. It's been a tad dull lately."

"You planning to do something about that tomorrow?" Dumont walked through with him to the living room and looked across to the store.

"We shall see. We shall see."

Evy followed with the popcorn. Dumont bent to take some. She slid the bowl out of his reach down the coffee table to Defoe. "Guests first, Daddy."

Defoe shoved the bowl back. "Cut it out, girlie. I gotta put up with snivelling all day long in that dung heap across the road there. I don't want to listen to it from you."

Dumont scooped some popcorn and pushed it back.

"That store," Evy said, "is jinxed."

"What do you mean? I always get a really good feeling from

hardware stores," Dumont said. "That one especially. It feels real somehow."

Evy and Defoe were silent.

"It's got the answers to your problems. The one little gizmo that will make everything better." He waited. Evy and Defoe exchanged guilty looks. "The washer for the dripping tap."

"Which you go to replace and the whole tap falls apart," Defoe said.

"The paint to brighten up your kitchen."

"Which is the wrong colour."

"Or spills on the new carpet," Evy said.

"Looks all streaky and blotched because you don't know what the hell you're doing," Defoe added.

Dumont raised a hand. "Stop."

Defoe's anger surfaced. "Or the smelly heap that crawls in all bleary-eyed wanting four cans of Lysol and you're not sure which smells worse, the piss in his pants or the Lysol oozing out of his pores from the day before."

Dumont's hand dropped.

"The dame with the sunglasses wants plaster to fill the holes in her wall."

Evy kept going. "There's some who swat their kids for nothing."

"You guys are disgusting. Evy, I'm ashamed of you. You too, Defoe. The world is not all shit." Dumont rummaged in a drawer. "And whatever you got going there with your rope and pulleys, you better not be wrecking my view. Your damn store is the brightest spot on Main Street. It looks like it belongs here, not in some gingerbread fantasy."

Defoe made a little bow.

"Hardware stores are places of secret surprises." Dumont shut the drawer and pulled open another one. "Except maybe for grocery stores, they're the last real stores left. The rest are only for decoration."

"What are you looking for, Daddy?"

Dumont looked at Evy in surprise. It was his own grandmother's voice he heard, irritated over his inability to see what was right in front of him. "Something Grandma gave me. For just such circumstances." He pulled out a soft leather sack. "Because, while you may have been giving your store a facelift, it sounds as if you've both been neglecting its heart and soul."

Evy clapped her hands. "Yes. Perfect." She grabbed Defoe's hand. "Come on. You got matches?"

"Somewhere. What you gonna do? Burn the sucker down?" She dragged him out into the cooling evening and waited while he unlocked his door. When they entered the darkened store, she stopped, quiet, just inside the door.

"You ready, Evy?" Dumont asked.

She shook herself, then closed her eyes. "Yup."

"What are you going to do?" Defoe asked again.

Dumont pulled out a tightly bound bundle of silvery green. "A match, *monsieur*?"

"We need to clear the air," Evy said. "Clear away all the broken thoughts. All the bad things people have been thinking about you."

"Evy!"

"Well, they have, Daddy. You've told me how we all have bad thoughts inside us and sometimes they get loose even if we don't mean them." She waved her hand around the men. Dumont knew she was offering him forgiveness. He looked at Defoe's unshaven face, his red eyes. And offering Defoe help. He hadn't realized how much the man had been suffering. He held out the bundle.

"What the hell." Defoe struck a match. Dumont held the tip of the bundle to the flame. It caught, flared briefly, then began to smoulder. Defoe sniffed. "You two are gonna get me busted."

Dumont held up his hand for silence. Starting at Evy's feet, he circled Evy's body three times with the smoking sage. She opened her eyes, took the bundle, and began a slow clockwise circuit of the store. Defoe followed Dumont up to the till where they could watch her. Every once in a while she would stop. She spent a long time beside the Lysol.

As the store filled with the smell of sweetgrass and sage, the men's thoughts wandered. Dumont remembered campfires, darkness, and sleepiness. He remembered his grandmother. He could see the angles of her old face in the shadows cast by his daughter's cheekbones as she continued the smudge. He wished he'd never said what he had about her mother.

Defoe didn't know what he felt. It was dark, he knew that; it was tightly sprung in his belly, and he was afraid of its release. It wasn't thought. It was something else. Sorrow. Loss. Love. Here. Back again. He would never admit it, but he felt its warmth.

Evy spent a long time at one far corner of the store.

"What's back there?" Dumont asked.

"Plumbing stuff. Pipe. Toilets."

"Maybe she's flushing out evil spirits."

"It's okay to joke about this?"

"A little."

"You Indian? I took you for a Frenchie."

"A little of each."

Into the silence Defoe spoke again. "Back there, that's where the Bennings used to keep the animals. Fish. Birds. Turtles. Hamsters. It stank. I gave them all away. Grand-opening special. Ugh."

Evy reappeared, thoughtful. She completed her circuit, smudged the two men, circling Defoe's heart twice. He flinched. She tucked the smoking stub into a jar on the counter, then pushed the door open. She went to the side door and pushed it open too. The air moved through the store as it hadn't in months.

"A fumigation," Defoe said. His voice was rough. "I got plenty of Raid back there. Didn't need to go to all this bother. Folks'll think I've started smoking dope." He cleared his throat. "Now are you two friends again? Can I get to bed? I've got to get a little shut-eye before my great unveiling."

"The day is galloping, Leonard!" Dumont yells across the deserted Sunday-morning street. "Unroll the suckers."

Defoe holds up a hand. "Give me five minutes. Then go down the back steps and walk around onto Twelfth. Go on, get inside."

Evy can barely contain her nervousness. She leaps around the living room on the furniture–from chair to couch to footstool to coffee table.

"Evy, stop. You're too big for that."

"What if it's horrible? What if they arrest him? What if he leaves?"

"Things change, Evy." Dumont walks back to the kitchen. "Look at you," he teases. "In no time at all, you'll be–"

"Don't." She is at his elbow, one hand rummaging in the cutlery drawer.

"Feeling up boys on that couch."

She pulls out a bread knife and waves it at him. He opens his arms wide, dark eyes sparkling. "And I'll set up that little baby intercom and listen to every squeal."

They both jump when one of the canvases unrolls with a final snap. Another follows, and another. Her father grabs her hand. "Let's go."

They run down the stairs and through the back alley so they can approach the store from Twelfth. They look at each other before rounding the corner.

Evy doesn't understand at first. A Loomis van. Lilac bushes. The old church. Then her heart almost stops beating. On his canvases Defoe has painted Twelfth Avenue continuing right through, past all the scrubby little houses, down to the highway, the mountain rising behind. Cant Hardware is gone.

Dumont lets out a war whoop. "It's perfect," he says, running across Main Street to slap Defoe on the back. "A nose-thumbing of eloquent proportions. You are a genius."

Evy's heart is cracking open. She feels herself being pulled into the invisibility she so often longs for. She remembers that day in the store when Jackie Fredericks looked right through Defoe at her. When Defoe became invisible, did he want to stay that way? To watch, unseen, to listen, unheard? It is one of her greatest fears and greatest desires.

She runs across to the two laughing men and flings herself at Defoe. He staggers at her sudden weight in his arms. "I don't want you to disappear," she cries. "Please don't disappear. I'm sorry I couldn't imagine anything for you."

"Evy, it's a joke, a great big wonderful joke," her dad says.

Defoe picks her up and looks into eyes the colour of a blue sky just before darkness. He wipes her nose with his sleeve. She smells the paint on it.

"No, no. You were right, Evy like a Chevy. Imagining is a fool's game. The trick is to see what's right in front of you."

A bell starts ringing. All three look up Twelfth Avenue toward the cemetery and the Evangelical Church. Another bell rings. The Christian Reformed Church. Dumont thumps Defoe on the back. "You had this all figured. Leonard, you're one sly bastard. I can't wait to see their faces."

"Quick. Over here." Defoe pulls them inside through a rectangle cut into the canvas where his door is. Through the lingering smudge of sage and sweetgrass, they cross to another opening where they can look straight out onto the street. Their faces appear in the rear window of the Loomis van that Defoe has painted going down the new Twelfth Avenue.

Another bell rings. They watch as the cars from the town's three biggest churches begin the drive to the highway diners for Sunday brunch, a drive that will bring them all down Twelfth Avenue to the stop sign across from what used to be Cant Hardware. Evy gets ready to wave.

A Fool's Paradise

Yves Dumont has been banished to the bench in the alley behind Leonard Defoe's hardware store while his daughter helps lock up. He squints through the midsummer sun at the three rogue spruce trees in the vacant lot across the alley, wondering how they've survived this long. One day a big enough wind will snag one and topple it through the tangle of hydro and phone wires onto the dumpsters and cars parked at odd angles to the grubby back doors of the Main Street stores. The tallest one might even hit the hardware store itself.

As the back door opens, two black shapes swoop down from the trees. Leonard Defoe squawks and hunches reflexively, hands covering the spot where his red hair thins to shining scalp. He's bright red, half angry, half embarrassed, when he slumps beside Yves. "They sucker me every time."

"You're lucky you don't hear them when they begin squabbling at four in the morning." Yves likes to draw an imaginary bead on the nest from the front window in the upstairs Main Street apartment where he lives with his thirteen-year-old daughter. He imagines borrowing a pellet gun, timing his shots for Friday nights when the young and not-so-young bucks rev their motors up and down Main Street.

"When do you leave for Saskatchewan?" Defoe asks.

"Saturday or Sunday."

Defoe jiggles the change in his pocket. "Can't figure why everyone leaves town for the only weeks we're likely to get decent weather. Six months of snow, two of mud and mosquitoes and then, *kapowee*, the locals leave and the town fills up with fools who think the sun shines all year long."

"Maybe they're not the fools."

"My point exactly."

"Jeez, Defoe, sometimes I'd rather try talking to Isaac over there. At least one of us would be making sense."

"Isaac, you mean."

"What did I just say?" Yves bends and picks up a handful of gravel. He bounces a piece off the centre spruce. "Speaking of fools, what's Walsh put Isaac up to?"

When Daniel Walsh opened A Fool's Paradise New and Used Bookstore beside Defoe's hardware store, he installed a clear Plexiglas arch over the back stairwell to protect him from rain and snow when he ducked out for a smoke. Since yesterday Isaac has been gluing tiny squares of turquoise tile and fragments of Noxema blue glass to the inside of the arch.

"Ask him," Defoe says as Isaac jumps out of the way of the opening door. Walsh steps out, a cigarette between his fingers, the match already struck.

"Isaac, Isaac, Isaac. Wonderful. Overwhelming. This is truly fabulous," Walsh says through his first inhalation.

Isaac waves away the smoke.

"Sorry, sorry, sorry." Walsh jumps out of the stairwell. "Ah, gentlemen, mind if I join you?"

Yves moves to one end so Walsh has to sit beside Defoe. Defoe enjoys anyone who doesn't fit the Main Street merchant mould, but Walsh's dramatic gestures and extravagant speech make Yves uncomfortable.

Defoe nods toward Isaac. "What did you do to deserve the honour?"

"Ah, the incomparable Isaac." Walsh's cigarette draws a star in the air. "He takes recycling to an advanced level. He showed up yesterday with boxes of glass and tiles and set to work. It took me a while to figure it out, but I think I have it. There's a poster in my store he's quite fond of. Gohar Shad's mausoleum in Herat." Walsh closes his eyes, leans back, and crosses his long legs.

Defoe bites. "What are you talking about?"

"Gohar Shad was a Mongol queen who ruled a kingdom in Afghanistan for sixty years. She built an enormous turquoise dome to cover the graves of her relatives. She joined them there after Tamburlaine's grandson executed her. He thought she was fomenting revolution in her eighties. She probably was. A wonderful woman."

Yves stops trying to follow Walsh's story. He tosses a piece of gravel high into the trees. One glinting black shape flutters its feathers and settles back on the branches.

"Isaac didn't get those tiles from me," Defoe says. "He robbing the competition now?"

"No, no. He got them from another wonderful woman. Carla Jarvis. Do you know her?"

Both Yves and Isaac turn to watch Walsh. Isaac squints into the sun, his blond hair spiky with dirt. Yves holds his breath because, for an instant, it looks as if he might speak. Isaac, who has never been heard to say a word. The gravel drops from the trees and bounces toward him. He turns back to work.

"Where did she get them?" Defoe asks.

"Her house. You know the one. Right beside the cemetery. She bought it from a divorcée." Walsh guffaws a great exhalation of smoke. "Isn't that a fabulous word? Divorcée. Right out of the early sixties."

"Carla," Yves prods.

"Yes, yes, yes. The Texas girl. Worked at Willow Elementary. Wonderful to Isaac."

Walsh inhales mightily and exhales through his words. "I saw him in the liquor store one Friday with enough returns to buy a weekend's supply of swill. But he picked up a bottle of Sawmill Creek Chardonnay. Quite a nice little wine. The clerk told me he did this when he was going to Carla's for dinner. She wanted him to know there was another way to drink."

"This has something to do with the tiles?" Defoe interrupts.

"It's all inventory to God's hardware man." Walsh shakes his head. "This divorcée, before the divorce, in a last-ditch effort to save herself from terminal boredom, redecorated the house. Poor thing. A lawyer's wife looking for chic in the backwoods." Walsh's hoots arouse the ravens to more fluttering. "The house has a big entrance hall."

"A cathedral entrance," Yves says.

Walsh laughs. "From a cathedral to a mosque. That Isaac doesn't miss a beat." He recrosses his legs. "One wall was covered in turquoise tiles with gold grout, the other in mirror tiles with gold streaks. To top it off, the long window beside the door was dark blue glass."

"Sounds okay to me. I sell a lot of that mirror tile," Defoe says.

"Carla said it made her feel like the milk in the Milk of Magnesia bottle. She took it all down but couldn't bring herself to throw it away."

"So? That must have been a few years ago."

"So. When her house got snapped up last weekend, even before the FOR SALE sign went up, she had two days to clear everything out. Isaac helped her, and voilà, the tiles found a home."

"She didn't seem much interested in yard work. Did she move into an apartment?"

Walsh turns and, for the first time, really looks at Yves. "My dear boy, she's gone. Skipped town. North to Alaska. She says she's going to complete the journey she began ten years ago." He stands and grinds out his cigarette. "We're going to miss her, aren't we, Isaac?" He touches Isaac's shoulder before turning back to wave. "See you later, gentlemen. I must descend the stairway to heaven."

His laughter is still lingering in the air when Evy Dumont opens the back door of the hardware store and waves a bank-deposit bag at Defoe and her father. "Done. At last."

Defoe groans. "In thirty minutes this disgusting child does, on her first try, what I still can't do."

She glares at Defoe. "And would have been done a whole lot sooner if you, Mr. Messy, hadn't stuck that Woodmere cheque in the refund envelope."

"Oh, no. Did you include it in the deposit?"

"Of course."

"Damn. It'll just bounce. Give me the bag. I'll fix it."

"Then your till tape won't balance with the cash."

"Relax, girlie. I'll just say I took out some cash. To buy you supper. To celebrate your success. What was it, about thirty bucks? That'll get us something pretty good. What do you say, Dumont?"

Yves's dark eyes are bewildered. "She's gone. Just like that."

"Who?"

"That Carla. Carla Jarvis. Your school secretary. She's gone to Alaska."

"It's summer, Daddy. Everyone's going somewhere."

"Not everybody," Defoe grouches. "Some of us have to keep this town running."

"Not on holidays, Evy. She's sold her house. She's gone."

Evy flips a piece of gravel toward Isaac. Barely pausing, he lifts a foot and hacks it back. She catches it and tosses it from hand to hand. "I was thinking how much I'd miss Eudora when I went to high school. But if she wasn't going to be there, anyway..." Evy shrugs. "Too bad. That's a cool dog."

Isaac keeps working, but Yves sees him nod.

⁂

It wasn't the dog that finally brought Carla Jarvis into focus for Yves Dumont. Or the fact that she was the secretary at Evy's school. He'd seen her often enough over the years when he went to pick up Evy or drop off her forgotten lunch. But it had always been the teachers he'd noticed–the older ones doubting his ability as a solo parent, questioning his daycare arrangements; the younger ones looking for a date and pumping Evy for details.

No, it was just last week that he really saw Carla. Something about the way she was leaning against her old dark green Camaro, a compact and stocky woman in jeans and a T-shirt, short red curls, diamond stud glittering in her turned-up nose, holding herself back from the party, saying something that made his daughter laugh. Evy, all elbows and knees, straight black hair, tiny top stretched over invisible breasts, bare midriff, short swirling skirt, and scuffed running shoes.

He wondered what the joke was as the school librarian, Philippa Newcome, steered him toward a big cottonwood, its bursting seed capsules dropping white silk into the glasses on the table beneath. Philippa wore tight cutoffs, a halter top, and gold thongs. Her earrings sparkled; her shining blond hair swung heavily, her perfume moving with it. As she plucked the steaks out of his hand, poured him a glass of wine, and inserted three fingers into the front pocket of his jeans to extract his car keys, he couldn't keep his eyes off the sweat shining between her breasts. When she walked away to toss his keys into a large bowl resting between the front paws of a panting Rottweiler, he was mesmerized by the careless knot at her neck, the ties dangling down her bare back.

"What's with the keys?" he asked her. She laughed and refused to explain. He gulped the wine and looked around at the people wandering in and out of the log house, others leaning against the railings on the big porch, a crowd shouting encouragement around the volleyball net set up on the side lawn. He recognized two of the men playing. He'd had his head inside the high school's photocopier when the big redhead shoved the smaller bald guy against the wall yelling that, goddamn it, he was going to get the copier first and get the fuck out of his way. Yves had taken great pleasure in slamming shut the machine's doors, unplugging it, and rising between them to say he needed to replace a part and would be back later.

What idiocy had landed him in the middle of Willow

Elementary's year-end staff barbecue? He liked to take his time angling his way into a party. Drink his first beer on the edge of things and nod to people walking by before deciding if and how to join the action. Instead, he was being towed around like a pet by the appetizing Philippa, who was introducing him to all these people he saw regularly when he came to fix their office equipment. None flickered an eye in recognition.

"Looks like Evy's abandoned you," Philippa said. "She's probably more comfortable with Carla. Kids are funny. They think teachers get locked up in a cupboard when school's out."

"She's a bit past that stage," Yves said. Evy was now petting the dog whose head poked out of the Camaro's window. As if she felt his gaze, she turned and waved at him. Evy hated any woman who noticed the wiry muscles under his T-shirt or the smile that rarely broke through his reserve. She especially hated any woman who tried to befriend her in pursuit of him. Like her school librarian. Philippa had no idea what she was up against, he thought as she pushed him in front of the group tending the fire pit.

"If you don't already know him, this is Yves Dumont. Say hi." Her laugh tinkled.

They looked at him. He bowed slightly and shrugged. She dropped his arm and bent over to lay his steaks on the grill. He forced himself to look away from the way her shorts tightened across her buttocks, the line of vertebrae disappearing beneath the waistband. The people across the fire looked down the front of her shirt, glanced at him, smiled at one another.

Responding to expectations, even his own, had never been one of his strengths. As the delicious aroma of chicken marinated in soy sauce and garlic, steaks encrusted with pepper, skewered prawns, and salmon all rose up around Philippa, Yves lost his appetite. He set down his glass, tapped his pockets as if looking for cigarettes, nodded vaguely at the people around the fire, and walked toward Evy.

"Your cruise control worn out already, Daddy?"

"Back off, Evy."

"It's charming to see you here, Mr. Dumont," Carla said, holding out her hand for him to shake. Her accent was faint, but he could hear the South in her voice. "Are you here in your capacity as father, or is Philippa's photocopier broken?"

"He's her date."

"Evy, give me a break."

"Ah. That explains it. They don't invite the janitors or the bus drivers. I get invited only because it's too complicated to organize the food list without my help." She laughed without a trace of bitchiness.

"You have the best dog, Miss Jarvis." With two careful fingers Evy stroked its forehead. "She has the softest fur right here. Feel, Daddy."

Yves looked into the dog's eyes. Brown. Calm. "Name's Eudora, right?"

"Well done. You've made an impression, precious," Carla said to her dog.

"She has the best eyeliner," Evy said.

"And it never runs, even when she cries."

"What could possibly make a pretty girl like Eudora cry?" Yves scratched behind her ears.

"Even classy puppies like you get the blues, don't they, Eudora?" Carla lifted the dog's chin and looked into her eyes. "But no matter what, you keep up appearances."

Evy joined in. "Her nails click on the linoleum in the office as pretty as high heels, Daddy."

"And her cuticles are always perfect."

Evy and Carla giggled.

"Why is she in the car?" Yves asked.

"Madam's Rottweiler is loose," Carla said. "It would probably kill her."

"Or bad dates."

"Shut up, Evy." Yves flicked her ear. He looked past her into the Camaro's dark wood and leather interior. "You have a beautiful car."

Carla stroked the fender. "Yes. My car is beautiful."

"Will you take us for a ride, Miss Jarvis?" Evy asked.

"Did you bring your bathing suit?"

Evy flipped up her skirt to show briefs the same lime-green as her top. "This is it."

"Mr. Dumont?"

"Sure. But please call me Yves."

"My pleasure. And I would be happy if you would call me Carla. Especially if you could give it a bit of a Cajun accent. When I was a little girl, pumping gas on the interstate between New Orleans and the oil-rig country in Texas, I used to dream of being carried off by one of those nice young French boys with the sparkling eyes."

"His eyes may sparkle, but he's one lousy date. That Miss Newcome is going to be ticked off."

"I'll blame it on you, Evy."

"Tell someone who cares." She opened the passenger door, flipped the seat forward, and pointed to her dad. He crawled into the rich smell of old leather and sat beside Eudora, who sniffed him delicately. "This car must be about as old as we are."

Evy bounced on the front seat. "Isn't it sweet?"

"A 1967 Camaro. A pleasure to drive, though you have to be careful not to get excited on ice," Carla said, fishtailing around a bend in the road and leaving the party behind.

They all laughed as the sweet smell of sticky cottonwood leaves blew through the car's open windows.

⁂

Evy blows a puff of air into her father's face. "Somebody's inviting us out to dinner, Daddy, and you're off in La La Land." Yves smells a mint from Defoe's candy jar on her breath. "You're serious, aren't you, Mr. Defoe, about taking us out to dinner?"

"I don't feel much like cooking, Evy, do you?"

"Nah."

"Alpine Noodle House?"

"Combination number five. With the shrimp."

"Front door locked?"

"Yes, boss."

Defoe tosses the bank-deposit bag inside the back door and locks the door. "I'll leave the ravens to stand guard and otherwise trust the good thieves of the town to thieve elsewhere tonight. Isaac, you want to come?"

Isaac keeps tapping tiles into place.

"Granny Wing always gives us too much," Evy says. "I'll bring him some out."

Yves hesitates. "You two go ahead. I want to ask Walsh something. I'll be right there."

"Sure. Scallops, right?"

"Right."

The afternoon sun slants rays into the stairwell. Isaac is transforming the Plexiglas into an evening sky. The blue begins a brilliant turquoise at the bottom, the colour of a sky this small northern town has never seen. As the tiles climb into the arch, he has added more and more pieces of the darker blue.

Isaac steps aside to let Yves through. Their eyes meet. Yves tries to hold eye contact, wanting to see what there is of Isaac to know. What there might be beyond the boy who sleeps rough, drinks, makes sculptures out of garbage when he's sober, and never speaks. But Isaac's eyes slide away.

Yves pushes the back door open, walks down a narrow hallway, and stops, not sure if he wants to go any farther. Thick incense, tinkling music, angels dangling on golden threads. And books. Shelves crammed with books, boxes spilling books onto the floor, counters strewn with magazines and books. Walsh turns from locking the front door. Yves steps farther into the store and sees the poster, the huge turquoise-and-navy-blue dome, its top eaten away. The sky turquoise behind it. "It's like that Mexican jewellery."

"Lapis lazuli, not turquoise," Walsh explains. "From the Latin for azure stone. The colour of the heaven."

"That tomb, how big is it?"

"I don't even know if it's still there. Could be blasted to kingdom come by now. But it was huge. Used to be circled by twenty-seven other turrets. It was a university, mosque, dormitories, the whole shebang." Walsh stands beside him, at least a half foot taller. Yves moves back. "To prevent fornication Gohar Shad married off her two hundred handmaidens to the students on the condition they continue with their respective tasks. They could meet one night a week. An enlightened woman."

"I guess. As long as the handmaidens didn't mind. She been dead a long time?"

"Over a thousand years."

"Too bad. I know a couple of priests should have met her."

"The pope himself."

"My mom would never tell me who my dad was. Used to send me to the priest if I asked too many questions." Yves is surprised to find himself telling this. His and Evy's secret. He tells her the few fragments of suitable memories he has of her mother or his own and she makes up ones about his father. Sometimes he's a trapper from Great Slave Lake. Sometimes he's an astronaut. Mostly he's Leonard Defoe, hardware store owner, neighbour, and the closest thing to family they have in this little town that showed up with a job for Yves when he and Evy needed one.

"Later, my grandma told me that could have been my answer, that my mother had made a lot of confessions around the time I started making my presence known." Yves can laugh now, but churches still make him nervous. The trappings of ritual. Of confession. The dark incense of the curtained booth. Perhaps this is what unsettles him in this musty store. "She called me one of God's children. Should be at home anywhere, she said."

"Are you?"

Yves shrugs. "Here. Saskatchewan. I don't know. We still go to my grandma's place every summer. Give Evy a break from my cooking." Yves picks up a cookbook from the shelf beneath the poster and flips through the pages. He stops at a photograph of a salmon. "But Alaska might be a change. Evy's never been out of Canada."

"But Saskatchewan is so full of history. I've got an old guidebook back here somewhere."

Yves grabs his arm as he moves toward the back of the store. "Do you know where in Alaska she went?"

Walsh stops, turns, and slaps his forehead. "Carla. Of course." He bows. "Forgive my obtuseness. I fear I am losing what few intuitive skills I once possessed." His long arms flop to his sides. "I never thought she'd stay as long as she did. She didn't have much use for this town."

"You said she'd started this trip ten years ago?"

"Where shall I begin? Where shall I begin?" He sits on the stool behind the counter and twirls it once around. His grey hair floats in curls around his head. His light blue eyes peer at Yves. "What are your intentions?"

Yves leans a hip against the counter. "I didn't have time to think about intentions. I barely started thinking." He sees a man stopped outside, looking at the books in the window. "She was here all this time, and when I finally catch on that she's, well, interesting, she's gone. She never said anything about going."

Walsh twirls again. "I have to think about this. When I first met her, the circumstances were professional. I have to think about what is private and what isn't."

"Professional? Like you don't talk about what books people buy?"

Walsh guffaws. "I forget. I forget. You weren't yet here. An Anglican priest, my good man. An Anglican priest."

As Yves tries to make sense of this, he realizes many of Walsh's mannerisms would fit perfectly in the pulpit. How the store is a sanctuary. How Isaac sees the essence of things. "You gave it up?"

"Had to. I liked it, hell, I loved it, and I've been told I did the best funeral going. But I was no match for the great river of dogma. It chewed away at the banks."

"Sorry. You've lost me."

"Rules, my boy. Rules. They're treacherous constructions. It was the rules or my belief. I chose my faith and to hell with the church."

Yves nods toward the poster. "What did she believe?"

"Gohar Shad? Allah, perhaps. Beauty, definitely. And the mind's creations."

The phone rings, slicing into Walsh's exuberance. Yves wanders through the store, picks up a book called *Haunts of the Black Masseur: The Swimmer as Hero.*

⁂

Carla had driven them away from the shaved lawns, around to the shaggy side of the lake.

"Miss Jarvis?" Evy asked. "Why did you get your nose pierced?"

Her fingers touched the stone sparkling above her left nostril. "My gran taught me to favour my best parts. After my car and my dog, my nose is the prettiest thing I've got." She waved stubby fingers under Evy's nose. The fingernails were gnawed. "Wouldn't put any jewels on these now, would you?" She stretched back her neck. "And I've got hardly any neck to speak of, so what was I left with? The cutest little nose in all of Texas." She wiggled it. "So I put my diamond there."

"Is it a real diamond?"

"You bet."

"Didn't it hurt?"

"No more than being born, honey."

Carla turned onto a rutted track overhung with alder. The trees opened to a small gravel beach. She shut off the engine and something like silence entered through the windows. A pool of silence rippled by the lapping of calm water against the land, by the ticking of the cooling engine.

Beneath his hand Yves felt Eudora's patience break. The muscles in her hips tightened, and she jumped into the front seat, across Carla's lap, and out the window. Evy laughed and climbed out her window, stripping off her skirt and throwing it on a branch. Carla opened her door. While she rummaged in the trunk, Yves folded his shirt and jeans on a fender.

The different ways people get wet: Evy dawdled, zigzagged across the gravel, and crouched to dangle her fingers in the water.

In the yellow boxers she had given him for Father's Day, Yves ran howling in with a huge splash, then looked back to see who he could torment. He hesitated. Carla picked her way on tender feet across the rocks. Her black Speedo emphasized the smallness of her breasts, the muscles in her chunky body. She entered the water without speed or hesitation and dived. She swam underwater, rising to breathe, then disappeared. Yves and Evy watched, wondering where she'd surface next.

⁂

Yves tries not to listen to Walsh's increasing agitation. Something about the homeless and tables in the temple, cash spilling to the floor. From the dusty look of the shelves and Walsh's threadbare shirt, not much cash is spilling in A Fool's Paradise. Yves picks up a book with a loon on its cover.

⁂

It was birds they'd ended up talking about when Carla finally rose beside Evy who was floating, her head on Yves's shoulder. Birds and summer.

"I could never get enough of the water when I was a kid," Carla said. "Once a year Gran would pick up me and my little brother and take us to the Gulf. She pulled a little tent trailer we'd live in."

"Sounds like fun," Evy said.

"It was what summer should be. Long days playing at the beach. Instead of what Momma had us doing. Pumping gas. Washing windshields. Changing oil. While she drank with customers in a little bar she ran out back."

"A gas station? And a bar? Together?"

"That's Texas for you, Monsieur Dumont."

"What about horses?" Evy asked.

"Not that part of Texas, honey. The outskirts of Beaumont. A ratty little place. Far enough from downtown that you could never get there. But not out in the country either. Motels, car washes, gas stations. Taco Bells. That was my neighbourhood. But no matter how much Momma howled she needed us because summer was the busiest time, Gran would haul us out of there."

A pair of mallards and four chicks paddled out from a clump of reeds. "Look, Daddy, look." The ducks hurried across the open stretch of water into a patch of yellow water lilies.

Yves lay back, floating. "I remember the ducks and geese back home, thousands and thousands of them, heading for God knows where."

"They knew where they were going," Carla said. "North. Where there isn't a human person for miles."

Yves closed his eyes. "Every year I'd look for the pelicans. Flapping like they were going to fall out of the sky."

"Pelicans!" Carla spluttered. Eudora looked up from the shore where she was waiting, head on paws. "You have pelicans up here?"

"Nah. In Saskatchewan. In the rivers mostly." Yves laughed. "People expect everything about Saskatchewan to be dull. They don't expect pelicans."

"I never would have," Carla said. "They winter in the Gulf. White in the sunlight on the water. One time Momma's boyfriend took us out of school and brought us down there in the middle of winter. He was cooking up some deal and wanted us along as cover. We spent hours wandering the beach, waiting for him. My brother threw rocks right into the middle of a big old bunch of pelicans and they rose up and wheeled around, squawking and carrying on. He always wanted to stir things up, that boy, get things moving."

"Your brother?" Evy was wistful.

"He finally got me moving even though he was still a baby."

"A baby?"

"In my part of the world, Evy, a baby brother is always a baby brother even if he's a foot taller and fifty pounds heavier. He was eighteen." Carla lifted one hand out of the lake and dribbled water onto her face. "We spent our childhood watching people pass through Beaumont, always on their way somewhere. Lots going to Alaska. We used to talk about a place where the sun never set, but the heat didn't fry you. It had to be heaven."

She rolled over and dived. When she rose, drops of water shimmered around her. "The Camaro was a sign, my brother said. It was meant for us. It sat in the parking lot for a week, abandoned. Someone's plans messed up. I don't know. We were like little kids. We'd go out and pretend it was ours. Pretend we were on our way somewhere. Momma was set to sell it off when we found the keys under the dash and took off."

"That beautiful car is stolen?"

"If someone left a baby on your doorstep and you took it in and cared for it, would you call that stolen, Mr. Dumont?"

"What about your granny? When she came to take you to the beach and you weren't there?"

"Evy, I swear you are the sweetest little girl I have ever met. I never would have left Gran. She had passed on by then. We had to make our own plans."

"Where's your brother now?" Evy asks.

Carla shuddered. "In Texas night comes early summer and winter, but the water is a lot warmer. I've got to get out of here."

They shivered in the bushes, wriggling into clothes stubborn against wet skin, slapping mosquitoes that moved between Evy and Carla on one side of the small opening and Yves on the other. He wanted to cross the clearing and join them in friendly and comfortable nakedness. Much more than he had earlier wanted to tug on the strings dangling from Philippa Newcome's halter top. He wondered if the years of looking out for Evy, of avoiding women like her mother, had turned him into a different man. If he'd been looking in the wrong places.

Sudden tears gathered in his eyes, surprising him. He imagined Carla as a girl, floating in salt water. He had never tasted the ocean, felt its salt drying on his skin. For an instant he felt the aching pull of gravity on the underside of his testicles, like the tug of loneliness itself.

⁂

Yves drifts back to the counter when Walsh hangs up. The phone call has squelched his extravagance. "Carla and her brother were on their way to Alaska when he got a bad headache, so bad she stopped at the hospital. Within a couple of hours he was dead. An aneurism. Stanley at the funeral home asked me to officiate. I was the nearest thing to an Episcopalian he could find. We buried him in the graveyard."

"Ten years ago?"

"Yup. She was about twenty-three. The kid was eighteen. I asked her if she wanted me to call her family." He imitates her accent. "'They wouldn't care to hear,' she said."

"Wouldn't care?"

"My question exactly. She said, 'You think I underestimate them? Believe me, Mr. Walsh, I choose my words carefully. My family would not care to hear.'"

Walsh turns back, elbows to the counter, head in his hands. "It sounds terrible, doesn't it? Unforgiving. It made me afraid for her. But I didn't ask again. I never could. She has a way of keeping you at a distance without ever being anything but warm and friendly."

He pushes back his stool and stands up. "I didn't think she'd stick around here, but then somehow she got a job, bought a house. After a while I didn't think about it at all. It wasn't until Isaac showed up with those tiles that I figured out what was happening. If I hadn't gone up to see her, I don't know if she even would have said goodbye."

Walsh suddenly gathers his limbs together and starts rearranging stacks of books behind the counter. "What am I doing? I've got a meeting in fifteen minutes. You'll have to excuse me." He circles the store, muttering to himself, flicking switches, unplugging some plugs, plugging in others, then disappears into a back room, knocking over a stack of empty cardboard boxes.

⸙

"Daddy, do you think the pelicans are happy in Saskatchewan?" Evy asked as they got back into the car.

"Well, they keep coming back. I guess you could say it's where they're from."

"Where are we from?"

"I'm from Saskatchewan, but you, you're pretty much from here, I guess. If you stay long enough in one place, that's where you get to be from."

"How did you end up here?" Carla asked.

"It just happened. When Evy came to live with me, I needed to get out of the bush. There was a job here. Seems okay."

"Do you ever feel like you don't really come from where you come from? Like you were meant to be from somewhere else?" She twisted to look at him, her damp hair flicking water onto his mouth. "How do you find your home then?"

Yves licked his lower lip. "Maybe it's where the people you care about live."

Carla started the car and backed onto the road. "This place gets to me sometimes. When school ends, I just want to get out of here. But I don't have any place special to go."

"There's always that. If you don't know where else to go."

Evy snorted. "I can imagine a million places I want to go. To Paris. To Australia. To the top of that mountain." She pointed to the round hump still speckled with snow, the ragged peaks glittering above. "If I had my own car like you do, Miss Jarvis, I'd be flying up that road this very minute."

"From what I've heard about the potholes on that road, flying would be your best bet."

"Very funny, Daddy," Evy flounced her shoulders. "What about Alaska, Miss Jarvis? Did you ever get there?"

Carla pulled in behind Yves's battered Honda Civic and reached over to open Evy's door. "It seems like such a long ways away, honey."

"But it's not, Daddy, is it? Not even a whole day. Just get in your car and go. If we weren't going to see my cousins, I'd come with you." She flipped the seat forward so Yves could get out.

"Oh, no." He patted his pockets. "That Rottweiler's got my keys."

"Why does the dog have your keys, Daddy?"

Carla was laughing.

"Why *does* she have my keys?"

"School tradition. All the keys in a bowl and anyone drinking too much can't have them back. You call a cab or a friend drives you home." Her smile grew. "Or you spend the night."

"How did I get into this?"

"Miss Jarvis, let's leave him here. This was all his big idea. We can get something to eat at A&W."

"Honey, I think you'd better be there to ride shotgun. He may well need your protection."

⁂

Her house was beside the cemetery's flat markers in a plot of grass and spindly trees. Yves hadn't known it was the cemetery. It held no significance for him. Neither did the house until he saw her in the yard. Cutoffs. Bare feet. Staring in her own front window. When he pulled the van into the driveway, she didn't recognize him at first.

"Any of your office equipment need tending?"

She surfaced out of some deep place and smiled. "Mr. Dumont, I do not have one piece of office equipment in my entire house. My phone has a rotary dial. Some days I am hard-pressed to find a pen and piece of paper."

He looked at her house, its slanted roof, blue paint, bare windows. It looked uninhabited. The lawn was full of weeds and needed mowing. He could see mosquito bites on her legs, dirt on her feet. She needed tending, he thought.

"You escape okay the other night?"

"Evy lifted the keys from the bowl while I distracted the dog with my dried-out steaks."

She laughed.

"Then Evy shivered pathetically. She's so skinny she worries people. We went home."

"Thanks for the swim. Not many folks around these parts swim. There is not much to beat the pleasure of floating conversation."

"Where's your car?"

"She's getting a full facial and body check in preparation for a little summer workout."

Yves heard his car phone. He didn't move. "You're going on a trip?" The phone rang again.

"Now don't let me keep you from your work."

The phone rang again.

"You all take care now."

She had stood on the lawn watching him drive away. Drive away from a house stripped and packed. Without saying a word.

⁂

Yves sets the tumbled boxes back into place and opens the back door. Instead of desolation, he is overwhelmed by blue. A blue that has deepened to a night sky into which Isaac is embedding splinters of shattered mirror and golden glass. Yves turns around and around. "Stars," he says.

Isaac, standing in the arch, is framed in sunlight. It flickers off the glass. Yves moves his hands over the walls carefully like a blind man conjuring up a path.

Walsh calls through the open door. "She wouldn't say much about where she was going, would she, Isaac?"

Yves brings his hands down from the tiles and looks at them as if expecting to see blood, visions. He steps into the sunlight and takes hold of Isaac's shoulders. "It's beautiful."

"She did say something about the midnight sun at Nome. Maybe it would illuminate things so she could see what to do next." Walsh sounds querulous. Isaac is smiling.

Yves turns to Walsh, who has come up behind him. "This is beautiful. What did you call it? The dome of heaven?" He grabs Walsh and begins to push the startled man across the alley in an awkward waltz.

The back door of the Alpine Noodle House flies open. Leonard Defoe shields his eyes. "My God, what do you call it when you get three fools together in the same place?"

"Only three?" Yves hoots back, still dancing.

Walsh is getting the hang of it. "One, two, three, one, two, three," he mutters, dipping and gliding.

"Granny Wing says if you don't come now, she'll feed your dinner to the crows and I'm still going to have to pay for it."

"Good for the crows. To hell with dinner." Yves stops moving and grins. "What say we fire up your truck and take Evy to the top of the mountain? Surprise the hell out of her."

"It's damn near seven o'clock."

"That gives us hours of daylight yet. This is the North, remember?"

"Okay, okay. Christ almighty, Walsh, whatever you got going there, it's bloody contagious. Look at Isaac. He's smiling."

Above the rising voices, the top boughs of the spruce start swaying and a dozen cawing ravens lift off. Out of their midst, two squalling fledglings cartwheel down through the air toward the men. Just as everyone ducks, the birds catch themselves and the men feel the swish of powerful wings ruffle their hair. The ravens gurgle deep in their throats and begin the climb to join the others already spiralling high above town.

Tending the Remnant Damage

The blast of the ship's horn woke Carla Jarvis out of a cramped sleep on the back seat of her Camaro down in the dark belly of the ferry. She struggled up, stretched, and crawled into the front seat. Looking at her face in the rearview mirror, she licked a finger, ran it over the dark circles under her eyes, and polished the diamond in her nose. Eudora licked her neck, the dog's breath a match for the taste of her own morning mouth. She brushed out her red curls and ran the brush through the fur feathering the tips of the dog's ears.

The ship groaned in its mooring, and car engines began to cough all around her. She started hers and followed a Toyota past three gesturing men in orange vests and up the steep ramp into the morning. She blinked in the sudden brightness. The road forked. A transport truck filled her rear window, its left signal flicking. She turned right.

The sun flashing on the water sent her scrabbling in the glove compartment for sunglasses. An ice scraper and her wallet hit the floor as she struggled to steer. Eudora whimpered. Glasses on, Carla looked for a gas station or rest stop. She needed to pee, brush her teeth, and get a coffee. In that order. Then figure out what she was doing here. Here was the Queen Charlotte Islands. Haida Gwaii. Every year the grade fours at the school where she had been secretary wrote reports on the Haida. Drawings of totem poles and killer whales down the long hallway. The ferry traffic pressed close, hurrying her along the narrow strip of highway. Nothing but trees on one side and ocean on the other.

Ahead, cars swerved out around a bent figure trudging along the pavement, shoulders pulled down by two plastic grocery bags. Longish brown skirt, pink socks, and white sneakers. A scarf.

The Camaro groaned and faltered as somewhere inside metal ground hot against metal. The smell of burning filled the car. Carla panicked when she saw the temperature gauge leap into the red, and pulled onto the crumbling shoulder, coasting to a stop behind the woman who turned, nodded, and walked toward the passenger door.

Carla jumped out. "I think you'd better stand back, ma'am," she said, opening the hood. Orange flames flickered through boiling smoke. "Stay back," she called again as she ran to flip open the trunk to get her fire extinguisher. Cars were pulling over now and people yelled. She looked up, fire extinguisher in hand, to see the old woman unscrew the lid on a big bottle of red juice and pour it on the smoking engine. Through the explosion of steam Carla heard a crack. A tide of voices rose around her as someone took the fire extinguisher from her hands and covered the engine with foam, as others gathered to pick the woman up from where she'd stumbled back. She was old and shrunken, but in the shrinking had stretched smooth instead of wrinkling. Under the scarf, scant black hair with wisps of white. Brown skin, brown eyes. Her voice came out of the murmurs, deep and clear and unperturbed.

"Did I bust it?" She pointed to Carla. "Should have told me you had that fire thing. Wouldn't have wasted good juice. Keeps my bladder clear."

Carla felt a hand patting her shoulder. She felt the sympathetic looks. She didn't know if the woman was joking. "Well, ma'am, if someone will be kind enough to get me towed to a garage, we can find out what the damage is. And then I'd be happy to buy you a glass of juice."

⁂

"Can I buy you a drink, beautiful?"

The Camaro glittering green at the gas pumps in the Texas sun. Her little brother behind the wheel, black hair curling, brown eyes sparkling, white teeth flashing. She wished for the thousandth time his father had been hers. Had passed on his slenderness, his olive skin. His daring. That someone like him would come along and buy her a drink, buy her a drink in some place far away from this little bootleg diner and gas station their mother ran.

"Hang up that gas hose and slide your big butt across this leather, turtle girl."

She did. Just like that. Slid onto warm leather, knees under polished wood.

"Where are we going?"

"Alaska."

⁂

A woman in her fifties, built like a tube with bulges for breasts and butt, climbed down from the tow truck. Terrier grey hair sprang out from under her peaked cap.

"Hey, Emma," she said to the old woman, "what kind of no-good nonsense you up to?"

"I busted up this nice girl's car. Her name's Carla."

Carla nodded hello.

"I hear you need a tow. Name's Bunny. As in Bunny's Beaters. Rent you a wreck while we fix yours."

And she cleared the traffic out of the way, hooked up the Camaro, waited while Eudora sniffed her carefully before jumping inside, loaded Emma and Carla into the tow truck, and drove them all into Queen Charlotte City. Carla was barely aware of the town unspooling between the water and the cliffs as Bunny questioned her.

"I was going to catch the ferry north, but the fishermen were blocking the Alaska boats out of Prince Rupert," Carla explained.

"Never good to stop a fisherman fishing," Emma said, scrunched between them. She smelled of wood smoke.

"You could have turned around, gone up the Stewart-Cassiar highway," Bunny said.

Carla laughed. "I thought the gravel would be too hard on my car."

"Where'd you start out?"

"Texas."

Bunny whistled. "A long ways to come. When did you leave home?"

"About ten years ago now."

Thirty seconds into the pause, Carla realized how crazy she sounded. "I haven't been travelling all that time." She named the small interior town where she'd been living for most of those years. "I kind of got held up."

"I'll say." Bunny turned into the parking lot in front of Queen Charlotte Automobile Lease and Service Centre, a sagging red garage with two decommissioned gas pumps. "You book a place to stay?"

"No, I, ah..." Carla climbed down and turned to help Emma, hoping a logical thought would wander by. But Emma had slid down right behind her and was already hollering at someone in the shop. A camper drove past. Islands in the channel rose green, then blue, and back bluer and bluer until they merged with the opposite shore. A kingfisher chattered. She hadn't heard a kingfisher since she was a child in Texas.

A huge man came out to whistle at the Camaro. "Wow. Don't see many of those," he said. "What is it? A '67?"

Carla nodded, the cadence of the voices around her as unfamiliar as if she had just crossed the border, as if she hadn't spent years submerged in their rhythms. Her heart thumped. She swayed as if she were still on the ferry, trying to keep her footing on a rough crossing.

"The girl's beat," Emma said, suddenly beside her, thin fingers strong at her elbow. "Take us over to my place until you get the car figured out."

⋙

As the Camaro sped north, he tossed sunglasses into her lap.

"Where'd you find these?" The red frames pinched her ears. The first boy she'd slept with had bought them for her from a beach stand at Port Arthur. She'd felt sick and hollow as she tried them on, afraid of what was coming but desperate to do it.

"In your closet. I rooted out a bunch of stuff you're going to need." He giggled. "Don't want to go snow-blind."

When they pulled into the first gas station, he stopped her from jumping out to tank up. His hand on her arm. "You don't do that anymore. Wait for it." They giggled as the old man hitched up his pants on his slow shuffle across to the pumps, leaned in, and asked their pleasure.

"Fill it up." His voice the raw deepness of an eighteen-year-old. Giggling as she asked the man the way to the toilet. A filthy, tilting shack, her thongs sticking to the planks. As she hovered over the fly-swarming blackness, she scrunched her toes so they wouldn't touch the floor.

⋙

The big man drove back out the highway until it curved north to go up island. He dropped them at a small cedar house, its siding weathered silver, the front deck hanging over the bank to the beach. Not another house in sight. Carla felt abandoned as he drove away, leaving her climbing stairs behind this old woman she didn't know at all.

When she asked for the bathroom, Emma pointed to a trail.

Carla walked into the darkness of overhanging trees until she came to an outhouse. Clean grey planks and the underlying odour. A bucket of ashes beside the small footrest. She sat and peed into the darkness, her tired, unwashed smells floating up around her. Wasn't there some story about these islands? Something about a stone. All alone at the edge of the world. It so perfectly described how she felt right then, she was surprised to find herself rising, using the toilet paper hidden under the coffee tin, pulling up her jeans, going back out into sunlight. Instead of sinking into blackness.

Eudora froze at the bottom of the stairs to Emma's house, hackles raised, tail high. A black dog growled from under the porch. Emma yelled from inside, sounds Carla could not turn into recognizable words. The dog backed farther into the darkness. Eudora jumped the bank to the beach.

"What's that you call your dog?" Carla looked in the open doorway. The cedar walls glowed amber. Red linoleum covered the floor under the kitchen table where Emma had set out a Styrofoam tray of muffins. An old maroon couch ran the length of a big window that looked over the porch onto the water. A small wood stove in a corner. A green velour curtain across a doorway.

"Only one around here listens to Cree language. If you want to call her something, call her Bear."

"Cree? I thought this was Haida country."

Emma ran water from the single tap into a kettle, plonked it on a propane burner, and took two cups from behind the patchwork curtaining the cupboards. "I'm a Plains Indian," Emma said. "We like a little space between us. After living in the village all those years, I got my boys to put up this place. Don't like that clutter."

She rinsed the cups. A pail under the sink caught the water that dripped from the drain. No chance of a hot shower.

⁂

The shower in the ratty motel outside Sherman washed away the dirty look the woman had given her when she checked them in. Looked out the window at the boy in the Camaro and then back at Carla's red sunglasses, piled-up hair, and short shorts. Carla had wanted to slap the crumpled face.

"No underwear," she said, sorting through her clothes.

"You think I was going to root through your lingerie?" He snapped the tab on a can of Dr. Pepper, slurped some, and poured in whiskey from a hip flask. "We can get some tomorrow. In Oklahoma. Okie undies."

"Where did you get the money?" She didn't really want to know. Coming home some nights with that bruised look. Shadows around his eyes. Eyes that weren't looking clearly at what was right in front of him.

"None of your beeswax."

⁂

Emma shooed her out to sit on an old car seat on the porch where the sun was starting to put some heat into the morning. She brought out a cup of tea and a couple of muffins. As she stared at the straight line of the horizon, the waves glittered and moved through the green water like wind through green fields.

Emma's rocking chair creaked. The muffin was stale and turned to glue in Carla's mouth. She forced herself to swallow.

"Hecate Strait," Emma said. "Closest thing to prairie you get around here. I wanted to look and see nothing but sky."

"In the town where I've been living, there's a big mountain. It occupies the sky like it owns everything." Carla's voice cracked as if she hadn't spoken in a long time. "I hate the sight of it."

Cars passed on the road above the house. Water touched the rocks. Air breathed through the trees and across her face, lifting her hair. Carla was exhausted, dislocated, yet oddly at home. Sitting with her grandmother beside the camper, watching her brother fishing in the Gulf of Mexico.

"Finally seemed like it was time to finish the trip," she said.

"To leave that mountain and get to Alaska." She was crying. "And then the blockade. And then the car. Like some cuckoo fairy godmother's been working overtime to mess me up."

Emma handed her a handkerchief and led her into the dark room behind the curtain. She pulled back the blankets on a narrow bed built into the wall, sat Carla down, and pulled off her shoes. Carla lay down obediently. She smelled old-woman hair on the pillow and didn't care. She let the residual rocking of the waves lull her to sleep.

⁂

They stopped in a little strip mall outside Ardmore.

"Love County undies. Just what you need to cheer you up."

She picked through the discount bin. Red, black, purple, and pink panties. Two lacey bras. He threw her a fifty.

They shot on through the searing heat and dust of Oklahoma until she made him stop in Norman to buy some lipstick because her lips felt like leather. Past the turnoff for the Will Rogers World Airport, past the National Cowboy Hall of Fame, across the Canadian River straight north.

He tuned the radio to some big Wichita station where they talked like Northerners.

"Time to get the South out of our talk, honey chile, or we'll stick out like dope in a potato patch. Now repeat after me. We're off to see the wizard. The wonderful wizard of Oz. Because because because because because..."

She was driving then, her new brassiere scratching her breasts. "Because," she sang along.

"No," he yelled. "Not cows. Caws." He flipped down his sunglasses and pushed his elbows out under his black T-shirt, flapping like a crow.

⁂

She awoke to voices. The wool blanket on Emma's bed scratched her cheek. Many voices. Cars. Eudora. Where's Eudora? And the dog was there, licking her hand. She climbed out of bed.

Combing her hair with her fingers, Carla pushed aside the curtain and looked into the empty kitchen. A little girl peered in the window and, seeing Carla, danced away. "She's up, she's up."

Cars and trucks were parked at all angles among the trees. In the yard a long table sagged under platters of food. "All my children's Haida relations," Emma told her, pulling her outside.

Carla was bewildered by their variousness. One woman so smooth and elegant she looked ready to host the national news. Another woman, her face collapsed, a tubby body in a T-shirt on top of the skinniest legs Carla had ever seen in black capris. One boy, slow and fat, eating steadily through a bag of Cheesies. A wiry, twenty-something tough whose hair bristled along white scars. Older men in windbreakers and peaked caps, their wives tending the food, hollering at the kids, teasing the young men and women.

"It's my birthday," Emma said.

"Well, happy birthday."

Emma shrugged. "They're counting me down. Now go eat. There's plenty of food."

Suddenly starving, Carla nodded and smiled her way through the curious looks and filled a plate. Salmon, potato salad, bean salad, mashed potatoes, sliced pork, green beans, biscuits–feast food. Near the end of every year, the Indian families at her school organized a feast and told the kids the Indian names for the rivers and mountains. It had sometimes made her want to cry, watching the serious little faces serving their giggling and awkward classmates paper plates of salmon and bannock. For a few hours allowed to be the hosts in their own houses.

She found a stump to sit on and tried not to gobble. The window girl slid like an otter through the clusters of people toward her. Her hands slipping across Carla's shoulders were hot and curious. One finger darted out to the diamond in her nose, then the girl twisted away. Carla kept eating. She wanted a glass of water, or better yet, of cold white wine. She could see nothing to drink but a vat of pink juice, the same juice staining the mouths of the little ones playing in the trees and on the beach. She felt very white and very alone.

⸙

Driving into Kit Carson County, he joked. "This here's Indian country," he said. "Better work on our tans." Called her a squaw. She thought it was funny. But the mountains stopped them both joking. He only relaxed when they slid out onto the Montana plains. They stopped in Shelby just south of the border.

She lay awake that night, wondering when he'd come back in from the bar. For the first time she was scared. On the maps in school Canada was the empty space between the lower forty-eight and Alaska. But it was another country with people who thought Canadian thoughts and lived Canadian lives. Had Canadian laws. The shabby little Shelby they'd laughed at with its neon and churches suddenly felt reassuring. Carla could imagine living in the motel, in the clean white kitchen, under the brown-and-yellow painting of a farmhouse and wheat fields.

⸙

Carla was helping herself to the birthday cake, trailing a line of chattering girls, when a voice rose in screeching fury from the back of the house, rose and mixed with a rumble of male voices. Three angry women stumbled from the trees, driven by ferocious jabs from a stick Emma held in one hand. Red wine splattered onto the ground from an upturned gallon jug in her other hand. The kids sucked in their breath and scattered.

One woman, older and sturdier than Emma, grabbed the bottle just as she was about to throw it, and hustled her, still squawking like a mad chicken, inside. Two big men tumbled the drinkers into the back of a pickup, yelling after them as the truck roared off. Women hurried to clear up the scattered remnants of dinner, directing some children to stack leftover food in coolers quickly pulled out from under the table, others to haul them to cars. The older woman came out of the house, slammed the door on Emma's yelling, stomped down the stairs, hefted a couple of big buckets into the trunk of an old Cadillac, and drove off. In fifteen minutes the place was empty, the dishes taken, the porch swept clean, the cars gone.

Carla looked down at the thick icing on the cake she no longer wanted. She wished she had a car to drive away in. She gave her plate to Eudora and bent her cheek to the dog's soft fur.

Emma opened the door. Carla climbed the stairs and sat beside her. She pulled a comb out of her pocket and tidied Emma's dishevelled hair, adjusted the collar of her blouse, and tucked her sweater down over her thin hips. Then they sat together on the car seat, looking across the water at a journey, a highway neither of them knew.

⁂

"Taking my sister to the powwow up the Milk River," he said to the woman at the border. "She ain't never been to Canada before." The South was gone. He sounded like the men in the bar last night. His Shelby Sunoco hat tipped to the lady.

Carla said nothing. She'd stashed her sunglasses, combed out her hair, and put on a long-sleeved shirt and a pair of jeans. But she still sounded like the South.

The woman laughed and waved them through. As soon as they were out of sight, he pulled into a green and golden field, unscrewed the Montana plates, and tossed them high in the sun. They flickered in the light, then angled sharply down into the wheat. He screwed Texas back on.

"Always folks from Texas, Florida, going to Alaska. People from Montana stay put. Now you can talk as South as you want."

"How do you know all this stuff?" she asked.

⁂

It was almost dark when Emma finally spoke. "My kids are no good. Like fat pigeon hawks on the bootlegger's leash."

Carla didn't know if she was supposed to say anything.

"The old people say the Haida were like my people. Hunters. To hunt well you need to know how to live right. To know the right way to behave. My kids, they don't know this."

Carla heard this all the time.

"Me and their dad. We lost them somehow. In between. Here, you go with your mother's family. With my people, you go with your father and his kin."

"That's Cree?"

"Saskatchewan Cree."

"You're from Saskatchewan?"

"Paradise Hill."

"You're kidding."

"What's to kid?"

"That kind of name means it's probably a shabby little flat place. Like Beaumont, where I'm from. Not a *beau* or a *mont* in sight."

"It's pretty country where I'm from."

"How'd you get here?"

"Woke up on the cannery train to the coast. End of the war. Not too many men left at home. Prince Rupert was full of soldiers. From Texas even." She laughed. "Damn fool me hops onto Charlie's boat and crosses that water. Swore I would never get on a boat again. Or touch liquor."

"Those yours, drinking in the back?"

"It's the Indian curse. Everyone is kin. Everyone's pain is your own. And there never seems to be enough joy to wash you clean of it."

Carla thought of the people passing through her mother's bar. The regulars. The oncers. She could never decide whether she preferred them drunk or sober. And none of them felt like kin. Not like her gran. Not like her brother.

⁂

The car must have been tied up in ugly business to be abandoned in a ratty little gas-up-and-dine parking lot on the outskirts of

Beaumont, she thought that last night in Montana. For a time she wondered if her brother had something to do with whoever left the car there. If he was on the run from more than their mother and petty crime in a no-account Texas backwater.

"Where are we going now?" she asked when he turned off the highway and bumped down a gravel road.

"Like I said, to the powwow."

And ahead, trucks and campers, tents and tepees bloomed under the surprise of cottonwoods, green and shining in a big bend of a river. Two days of drums, dancing, and sleeping in the back of the Camaro. He disappeared for hours, then showed up with plates of food like the forgetful host of a party he'd thrown especially for her.

⋙

Bunny's truck bumped down the driveway early. She brought Carla a coffee, lit a fire to take the chill off the cabin, and put on the kettle for Emma's tea. She groaned as she bent to sit down. "Your Camaro's not the only thing that's toast," she said, rubbing her knees. She took off her hat and pushed the hair back from her face. She looked like a tubby cherub, light illuminating the white tips of hair, the red veins in her cheeks. "Knocked a hole in your radiator somewhere. Wasn't big, but it had all night on the ferry to drain. Then when you drove it, well, a basic case of barbecued engine."

Carla was numb.

"I phoned around and the nearest motor's in Edmonton. Cost about five thousand by the time it's here and installed. Then there's a lot of rust underneath. The body's about had it. Whoever painted it for you just covered the rust."

That car needs tending, her brother had said. And she'd tried. She'd had it fixed whenever there was a rattle, changed the oil, tuned it up, driven it carefully. Resisted all the offers to buy.

Emma shuffled into the kitchen, red wool shirt over a flannel nightie and long johns. She clattered dishes, making tea, slicing bread, setting out jam. "Don't know why I gave up drinking, the way I feel some mornings."

"Got some leftover ribs from the takeout for Bear," Bunny said.

Carla could hear the dog gnawing the bones under the house. Bunny tossed one to Eudora, who caught it lightly in her teeth and settled beside the stove to work it over. Then Bunny hefted something out of her jacket.

"Found this strapped to the frame when we lifted the engine." She banged an oil-stained plastic bag on the table. Her voice was edged with suspicion. "Wouldn't mind seeing what's inside."

Carla slowly peeled the brittle plastic from the bundle. Underneath, pale leather. As its cool weight settled in her hand, Carla remembered crouching in the dark outside a motel with her gran. She was a little girl, her brother asleep in the car. Gran had given her a bundle, a similar weight wrapped in soft cotton.

⁂

"This is where we made your momma," Gran said, digging under a dying bush.

"In the dirt?" Carla was disgusted.

"No, no. This place. I was misbehaving with your grandpa's brother. Doing my own fool bidding. That's where your momma comes from. One fool moment and the men are gone. We're left tending the remnant damage. My precious girl."

Carla didn't think there was much precious about her momma. Not since her brother was born. She'd let him cry, slap Carla for wasting diapers if she changed him too soon.

"She loved his daddy too much," Gran said. "Now we've got to do our best to keep loving her."

Tin flashed in the neon light blinking over the motel office. A tiny heart dropped to the bottom of the hole. Then the bundle. As Carla tipped it into the ground, she saw more metal flash. The barrel of a small gun disappearing under red dirt. Carla was afraid then.

"You and your brother," Gran said, "you've got to try your best to be something besides damage."

⁂

Carla's hands shook as she unwrapped the leather. Emma drew in her breath when two smaller bundles appeared. She moved her hands toward the braided grass that encircled them and lifted it to her nose. Carla could smell its sweetness. Before she could unwrap the next bundle, Emma put her strong fingers on the back of Carla's hand. She was suddenly fierce. "You're not having your period, are you?"

"No. Why?"

Emma relaxed. "Just checking. If it's what I think it is, you shouldn't be handling it when you're bleeding."

Carla unwrapped a stem of pale wood with a narrow hole drilled through it. As she lifted it, long feathers dangled from the beaded leather wrapped around it.

"Pelican," Emma said, stroking the feathers. "The male part is fancy, all decorated up."

"What's this to do with you, Emma?" Bunny asked.

"Just wait," she said. From the other wrapping she drew out a dull red tube with an upright funnel that looked like the smokestack on the ferry that couldn't take Carla to Alaska. "The female part." She put it into Carla's hands. "The part that lasts forever."

Carla was surprised at the stone's smooth weight. Two carved lines around each end. She lifted the bowl to her nose. Tobacco. Her brother was always encircled in a halo of smoke. Her eyes filled and she handed the pipe back.

"What was it doing in your car?"

"My brother might have put it there," Carla whispered. "It could have been someone else. I don't know."

Bunny broke in. "Emma, what are you on about? I thought it was a gun, for Chrissakes. It's only some kind of hippie hash pipe."

"It's a Cree pipe, a woman's one. An old one, like my mother's.

We use them to offer respect to the spirits. If I'd have stayed where I belonged, I'd have had one like it. Its rightful owner would never leave it in a car like that. Something bad happened for her to lose it." Emma looked at Carla, accusing.

Carla broke apart. She yelled, "I don't know what happened. I never knew and I never wanted to know."

⁂

The car hood slamming shut startled her awake. Her brother's hand was on her mouth, pulling back her blanket.

"It's just me. Time to go." He pulled her up. "You drive. Quietly past the gate and up the road. I'll just slide under this."

She climbed into the front seat and drove as he said, blinking sleepily at the men with flashlights, saying she had to get an early start. Monday morning, she said. You know what it's like. And then out the gate and she was awake and they were driving north through Alberta on their way to Alaska.

⁂

"Why don't you take it, Emma?" Carla suggested. "A birthday present, let's say. I don't want anything to do with this. It scares me."

"It's right that you're scared. These things can do damage. Most likely has done."

Carla could see it unrolling as if she was back in it. She could smell the malt balls he'd been eating, feel the stitching on the steering wheel sticky under her fingers. The pipe riding under the hood. Another one of his dirty little secrets. The ones she didn't want to know about. She began to speak.

"We came over the top of a big hill, and there's this valley with mountains all around. His head felt funny from the altitude, he said, like it was going to pop. He stared at this one mountain getting bigger as we drove west. He said it was trying to get inside his head and that's why he had a headache. He swallowed a handful of aspirins."

Eudora placed her head under Carla's hand. Her fingers scratched and stroked.

"I told him to sleep, but he said the only way for it to get in was through his eyes, so he had to keep them open wide. It hurt way more, he said, but the pain would be over sooner, over when the whole mountain was inside him."

Her voice faltered. The dog leaned against her knee. "I drove as fast as that Camaro would go until we crossed a river and saw the green *H* and turned and there was the hospital. He wouldn't get out of the car because the mountain filled the sky. He screamed when the nurses came out to get him. He screamed and said it wasn't done, it wasn't done, and they were going to drag the whole thing back out and it hurt too much, please stop. But they didn't. They put him on a stretcher and took him inside. Once he couldn't see the mountain, he relaxed. He was only eighteen and he told me not to worry, there was enough money under the back seat to pay. And then, smiling like when he was a baby, said, 'Oh, that's a beautiful mountain,' and closed his eyes." She snapped her fingers. "Gone. Just like that. My baby brother brought me all that way, then, with his head full of rock and snow, drowning in blood, left me. All alone."

The wind moved through the trees. Carla heard the sound of her heart pounding, the waves rising with the tide. Bunny handed her a tissue, and she blew her nose.

"He pried me loose of my momma. If it hadn't been for him, I'd still be down in Beaumont pumping gas and serving drinks to truckers. Probably have a couple of little trucker's bastards of my own. But then he left me alone. Alone with that goddamned mountain."

⁂

Carla is not going to Alaska. She is not driving the Camaro. She's in some new blue thing and she's driving it to Saskatoon for one of Bunny's customers. This dashboard is moulded plastic. A wide blue expanse between the wheel and the windshield. Power windows.

As she drives through the town she lived in for ten years, she plays with the buttons, makes the windows go up and down. Locks the doors. Unlocks them. She presses the Seek button for the radio receiver. Seek. It is a word she would like to teach Eudora. Find me, Eudora, for I am lost.

As she begins to retrace the road she travelled with her brother, she catches herself hoping that the years have been an illusion, that rewinding the film of that terrible day might bring him back. But she feels Emma's eyes on her shoulder blades. And no matter how stubbornly she resists such thinking, the pipe in the basket stowed on the floor behind her seat is as palpable as Eudora's soft breath at her neck.

"If it goes back where it belongs, maybe you can see past the damage, see through to some little scrap of a life," Emma had said.

Some little scrap of a life. Carla ponders this as she drives the long highway beside the upper Fraser River. A life of her own, without her brother, without the mountain, without Alaska. She tries to dream this life when her eyes refuse to stay open. When she sleeps in the car. The pipe and the dog breathe with her.

Then the mountains disappear and the land seems to roll its shoulders in long, slow sweeps, clearing itself of their weight. Carla's neck is stiff and she rubs the tight spot where she feels Emma's will bent upon her journey. She passes through Edmonton in under an hour, through the little towns, and into a wild night of lightning flashing from horizon to horizon. Outside Lloydminster, a huge refinery flames into the black sky.

By morning she has found the place Emma told her about, and climbs to the top of a knoll. Down below, a froth of poplar leaves shimmering in sunshine. Horses grazing. "Open it up to the sun first," Emma said. "Let it feel that hot Cree sun. Then," she told her, "dig deep." They walked the beach together below her cabin and picked a stone to mark the pipe's burial.

Carla wipes dirty hands on her jeans and unwraps the pieces. Buffalo calf leather, Emma told her. She suddenly longs to join the stem to the bowl before she rewraps them in their tender and separate skins. She doesn't know where the urge comes from, the pipe itself or her own loneliness, but Emma has forbidden her.

A magpie floats into the tree above her. Carla looks into its sideways bright eye. "Okay, okay," she says, and rewraps the separate pieces, places them side by side, and wraps them again. The tobacco smell of her brother rises from the skins. She cries as she covers them with dirt and plants the stone still sticky with salt. She feels a great tiredness as Emma's attention slides away and leaves her alone with Eudora's nose at her neck, tongue on her own salt-streaked cheeks.

⁂

"I feel like a scrap of cloth on the remnant table," Carla tells Bunny on the phone. "Some colour gone hopelessly out of fashion."

"I have a daughter, she makes beautiful things out of scraps."

"Thank you." Carla leans her forehead against the dirty glass in the phone booth and looks at the wide street, the angled cars pulled into the shaded side. "You are a kind woman. How's the Camaro?"

"Emma had it towed down beside the house. Someone gave her a couple of chickens. That's where they live."

"Ah, shit."

"Exactly."

"That woman was after my car all along."

"One of her grandkids is already spending time there. Has his eye on it."

"I did what she asked."

"Good. I'll tell her."

"I'll drop off the car in Saskatoon tomorrow."

"Great. Thanks."

"You too."

Carla listens to the dial tone, then steps out into the heat. She envies the kids playing fetch with Eudora, running and splashing in and out of the wading pool in the town's small park. She whistles and the dog comes.

She will have to buy a car in Saskatoon. Get Saskatchewan plates. Saskatchewan. What a lovely word, she thinks, rolling her tongue around it. What in the world does it mean?

Cultivation

The cows are in the uncut hay field, and at first, because I'm not paying attention, I think they are shadows at the edge of my vision. But I see the grass trampled, I see the cows chewing and looking right back at me. He keeps driving, but he's looking too.

"Have you seen Nadia lately?" I ask a half mile later at the mailbox.

"No." He struggles out of the cab and fights with the lock on the box.

"Me neither," I say as he climbs back in. I sort through the letters and flyers, the appeals for money. It's all for him.

I wait in the truck as he hauls the groceries into the house. Only a couple of bags. I see how carefully he comes back down the stairs, knees stiff. He slams the tailgate shut.

It's my turn. Another bag of groceries.

"She'd never turn those cows into the hay field like that," I say as we pause, breathing hard, at the top of the steps.

He takes out his handkerchief and wipes his forehead. It's the first real heat of the year. "Maybe it's a new kind of farming. Some organic technique."

"Never," I say.

"Remember how Wilhem cut half his hay last year, left those long strips of high grass? We all thought he'd been smoking pot on the tractor."

I snort.

"Said it was a way to return organic matter to the soil when you aren't running cattle." He puts his handkerchief away.

"Never, never, never." I pour cream in the coffee he gets for me as soon as I settle at the table, coffee he times to be ready when we get back from town. "Under no circumstances. It's too wasteful. They trample half of it. She'd never do it." I scrape at a patch of dried milk left on the table from breakfast, a spot the cloth missed.

He settles back in his chair, cup in both hands. "So, are you saying those cows in the hay field have some significance?"

"I bet she's left."

"There you go, jumping to conclusions."

"I wonder if she's okay. I mean, why would she go without those cows?"

"You stay out of it, honey. If they've got troubles, they've got them. And the cows have already done the damage."

"From what I heard her say, she preferred the company of her cows to almost anything." I haven't talked to Nadia in months, yet I find I'm worried. I don't know why.

"Whatever it is, it's done."

I can tell he's uneasy, doesn't know why I'm upset. He's counting the hours since my last medication.

I laugh, still scraping at the milk. "What could I do anyway? I have no experience with marital disputes, do I? I wouldn't know what to say."

And the pleasure in his smile says he knows I mean it. We are a good couple. We get along. All my disputes are with myself. He watches and waits, as he has been for months now. I don't know how much longer he's going to be able to wait. I take my pills, and he helps me to the couch. He moved it into the kitchen right beside the wood heater after Christmas, after that long cold spell. I couldn't get warm.

I lie there and remind him where to put the groceries. His back stiffens. I can see him figuring how to ignore me. Because he's getting his own system now, one he can handle. He's not restricted by tradition, by what we women see in all those visits to other women's kitchens. He's moved just about everything out of the bottom cupboards. Soup tins, glasses are in drawers. It makes sense. He doesn't bend very well. He wants to get help: home nursing, homemakers. But I want to wait until winter. Maybe then.

So I don't say much. I look outside and watch the grey jays tend their nest, trying not to think about how bare the shelves are looking, how thin we're both getting. I watch until shadows at the edges of my vision take shape.

A woman wanders idly through an empty house. She is thinking of her cows, of the cold spring nights walking the heat-sucking cement floor of the barn. The smell of hay and manure. The intimate smell of birthing, the same for all mammals. The heat of the fluid as females are pulled inside out. Wet curly-haired calves steaming in the still night air. Spring water running, mud squelching under rubber boots.

He comes in from his morning walk to confer before he goes to town. He will fill my prescription, have coffee with his friends, pick up the mail. Neither of us is up to my going along anymore. His kiss is as comforting and familiar as this house. He smells of cottonwood and coffee. I don't know what the house smells like. I haven't been out of it for days now.

I watch the truck turn out the end of the driveway. I make my way to the couch and stretch out as best I can in the sweet morning sunshine. It reaches into every corner of the house this time of year. I know the dust is creeping in too, creeping in from the edges of my house, probably creeping past the boundaries of propriety. But I want to keep it all to myself for a while yet–want to wrap it around my fear and pain like an old blanket.

I only care, really, when company drops in on sunny days. When I know it's all perfectly visible. But the only company we get these days is the Jehovah's Witnesses and the telephone man. He's trying in vain to get the buzz out of our line. It makes conversation difficult, the buzz, but secretly I like it. The distance and wires come alive. I can hear my voice running under poplar branches, over hay fields, pine flats, across the river to town. It's only right that it picks up some noise along the way.

As for the Jehovah's Witnesses, it's not entirely clear to me what they're trying to do. I like to feed them, to disarm them with neighbourliness and personal questions, but all they get now are Dad's cookies. They come once a month; each time they look at me more and talk less.

"She turned those cows out herself," he tells me later that day.

For a minute I don't know who he's talking about. I forget things are happening beyond these four walls, beyond the view from the window.

"She'd decided to leave and there was no one to feed them. While her husband was out of town."

"Afraid of him probably."

"Afraid? Of him? Why would she be afraid?"

"Had to get it done before she lost her nerve. Made it impossible to turn back, I'd think. Opening that gate. Shooing them out."

"You always assume these things. She's no chicken."

"But he's awfully persuasive," I insist, remembering his smooth, handsome face.

Just last fall he almost convinced me we'd be better off in town. Was ready to put in a good word for us at the lodge. He's on the board. I thanked him politely for his concern. But as I watched him drive away, I was disgusted, mostly with myself. He had me considering something we'd agreed never to do, my husband and I, and this was in a conversation at the mailbox, just casual conversation.

"I'd think she'd want it done. Irrevocable," I say.

I can see he's thinking now, remembering conversations he's had with him. There's nothing you can put your finger on; he's polite as pie, but you always leave dissatisfied, unsettled.

"Maybe you have something there. I heard he was pretty mad when he did get home."

I wait for it.

"I guess she'd done a load of laundry before she went, and left it in the machine, still wet. What made him maddest, he told the girl at work, was she'd left a couple of his silk shirts in there–you know how he likes to get dressed up–and they sat for two weeks. Now he can't get the rotten smell out of them."

I laugh. "And I always thought I was the only dolt to forget about laundry. It's not really automatic at all."

"Laundry," he groans. He hates it. It confuses him, dirt you can't see. The sheets get so musty I start to pull them off before he'll wash them. He says he doesn't notice the smell, the sweat.

"It was an irrational act," I say, "committed in a foolish moment."

"What? You think she left those shirts in there on purpose?"

"No, the cows. Why didn't she take them with her?"

Then I realize I don't know where she lives now, where she's spent the past month.

"No fences there, I guess. All that land is just for show," he says.

"Where are we talking about?"

"She's camped out at the old Newton place."

"Camped out?"

"I guess they still have to fight about the furniture."

"Were they running a workshop on this poor woman at the coffee shop this morning, or did someone call a press conference?"

He laughs, sheepish.

We sit down to dinner. He's happy I've been able to cook. It's been a good day. But the chicken has no skin. And there's no butter for his roll, only low-fat margarine. He looks at me, face serious, lined. "I don't know why you still bother with all this stuff. I have no intention of hanging around after you..."

My heart squeezes, my stomach flips. Fear and love both. "Just keeping you healthy until then," I say.

He's lying though. He will manage without me, will blossom under the tender ministrations of widows.

"I love the skin," he says. "It's the main reason I eat chicken."

"You love the fat under the skin. It drips down your chin." I try to laugh. "But you're right. It does seem dry and tasteless. There's probably a better way to do this."

I lay down my fork, tired now and upset. It's the first meal I've put together this week.

"Oh, honey, I'm sorry. What an idiot I am. I just..." He stops. "I can't keep it all organized. I can't take proper care of you. You're not even clean enough. I forget to wash the sheets, I don't wash the shirts so they come out soft–your poor skin is starting to peel."

I won't listen, pick up my fork again. "Why do you think she left him in the first place?"

He looks at me, helpless.

"I mean, no one seems surprised. I know I'm not. He's so smug. But I wonder what really happened to make her finally do it."

"Who knows?" He begins to eat again.

It's a mystery imagining people's lives. Imagining the sensory push beneath the reasoning, the impulses jarred by blue eyes maybe, or the smell of watermelon. Who can possibly know what they are? I still can't figure out why I get mad watching him hang pants up by their legs instead of the waistband. Or why the smell of turnips makes me want to cry.

She walks to the window above the kitchen sink and looks out, out to where the barn should be. But this is a different view. There is only scrub willow, brown grass, and the remnants of a small rock garden under a lone spruce. She wrings her hands, then jams them into the pockets of her apron. They are sweating,

and she feels her heart thumping.

She looks at the calendar she brought from home and hung up beside the sink. Her husband's shifts are marked right up until Christmas. Behind the calendar the wall is splattered with old water stains. The stove is greyed from idleness, the fridge smells stale. The worn checkered linoleum needs scrubbing. Three old potatoes sprout in the back of a cupboard with a tin of tuna and a jar of instant coffee. Somehow she can't cook, can't clean, can't organize. She has nothing to pattern her days by. She paces from the window to the door and back, then throws on a sweater and goes outside.

⁂

The wind is blowing today. I hear it before I'm all the way awake. From my bed I see the branches tossing, the leaves showing their silver underbellies. There's something about these late-summer winds makes you want to fling your clothes off, bare yourself, blow the dust right out of your navel.

The wind is still gusting in the evening. I want to walk out into it, get to some high place, feel it blow over me.

"I can see why people want their ashes scattered in the wind," I say, startling him. We don't talk about this part. "But I'd like somehow to be solid, something the wind blows up against, curls around."

He thinks. "Can't see how."

"No. Me neither. It's a good thing they didn't have kids," I add.

He's rattled now.

"Nadia, I mean." He doesn't want to talk about this either, and I don't know why I say it.

"I guess it makes the fighting worse, the bitterness..." I venture, then change my mind. He's used to this. "But Edna and Albert probably did better than some because of their kids. They were good to them even when they weren't good to each other." I wait, then try again. "Some kids seem to bring maturity to couples–like grandparents reincarnated to straighten out messes."

He won't be drawn in. He straightens the kitchen and talks about other things: the details that occupy his days now the animals are gone, the fields rented, the garden beyond both of us. I can see he's tired though. He sees the dinginess, even though he doesn't know where it comes from. We are going to need help.

He agreed to no children, but never really figured I would stick to it. I finally convinced him, but I saw then he was afraid of me just a little. Uncertain about how far I'd go. I liked that. I was curious myself.

It wasn't such a bad idea. I imagined a life of farming, of farming politics, of intelligent activity that kids didn't seem to fit into. But I was naive. I had no idea what kind of feat it would have been to get through all those years without getting pregnant. I got pregnant.

It was my turn to be afraid then. What could I do? How far would I go? We both knew I could have an abortion, and we both knew our marriage wouldn't survive that. We knew that without once talking about it. This huge silence between us.

I didn't have to tell him; he likely knew before I did. He's the sort of man who sees all the details of a woman's daily existence. He's politely curious. "How does this feel?" he will ask me when we make love. "And what about this?"

But I was so physically sick, I couldn't bear his touching me. He blamed himself. Without once talking about it, I knew that.

Then one morning, after he'd gone out to feed the cows, I fell back to sleep. I had a dream. I saw a young child walking in the horse pasture. I don't know if it was a boy or girl. It was walking away from me, snapping off fuzzy fireweed seed plumes. Our old horse, Nellie, was poking along behind, nibbling the stems.

When I woke up, I lay still and remembered the dream, remarkable for its uneventfulness. It was just that I was finally able to imagine this child in our lives. And I realized I didn't have to make a dash for the bathroom. I had finally stepped off that pitching boat of nausea onto sweet dry land. It felt so good to lie there, waiting peacefully.

By the time he came in from feeding the cows, the cramps had started. When it was all over and he sat in the hospital room holding my hand, his face buried in the pillow beside me, I knew he thought I was relieved. I knew he'd never believe me if I tried to tell him otherwise. He'd think I was trying to comfort him.

He wouldn't take chances after that. I try not to think about what a help a couple of kids would be right now.

The wind is from the northwest and bites right through the heavy sweater. Her hands, softened now except for the raw-bitten fingernails, redden quickly. They smell of nothing. Absent is the overwhelming odour of the lanolin cream she used before checking cows. She would smell it when she ate sandwiches, when she blew her nose, when she brushed her hair.

Her fingers remember the feel of the vaginas, calves' heads, sharp, wet hooves, hot, hot limbs tangled, sorting, pulling, twisting, her fingers deft, helpful.

She twists them deep in her pockets, the apron still hanging below her sweater. Now they stumble over buttering bread, buttons, over car keys.

Supper this time is from a can. Stew. But the carrots are fresh, from a neighbour's garden. Neither of us says much about the stew or the carrots; we miss our own cows and we miss our garden.

"She's not alone," he tells me.

"Who?"

"Nadia."

"What do you mean? He's at the ranch. The cows are there. Don't tell me he let her have the dog?"

"There's someone living there with her."

It's always a story with him, a story drawn out line by line with questions. I persevere. "Who?"

"Jack Edwards was up there hooking up the phone. Told his mom."

"Who?"

"Evelyn Landings."

"Evelyn? You mean..."

He waits, a grin on his face as I struggle.

"You mean, that's why...?"

He leans back. "And the brother."

"Not Johnny?"

"That's it. Johnny."

I stop there. It takes a whole glass of water to get the stew going right way down. The coughing hurts so much I can't finish.

I watch him clear away the remains of dinner as I wait for the pill to take hold. When it smoothes down the edges of pain, I say, "I could understand Evelyn...just maybe. But Johnny?"

Johnny Landings is a caricature of a sleaze. He's oiled his way in and out of dozens of unsavoury relationships. It's impossible to imagine anyone who's been here as long as Nadia doesn't know about him.

"Who knows what's really going on?" he says. "It's got most folks beat."

⁂

When she turns from the window, comes in from a walk, whatever does she see? That man, Johnny, leering at her buttocks, her breasts? Does he lean against the door frame, watching her, wondering how he can work this arrangement to his advantage? Or does she fumble her clumsy fingers over his body, pull at his clothes? Maybe it's as simple as lust. Maybe her husband was...inept.

⁂

On the way up to bed he stumbles. We both lose balance and he can't catch me. The pain as my hip hits the stair makes me cry out. I hear him yell, angry, but I can't make out the words. My ears are filled with roaring.

I look at him, weeping now on the top stairs. I can see his tears pooling on the worn wooden treads, treads I remember sanding thirty years ago. "That fir will last," the builder said. "It's expensive, but it never wears out." The stairs haven't been scrubbed in years.

I'd asked a lot of this man, I finally realize. More than there was any need. I pull myself over to him. "Sweet boy," I say, kissing the thin hair on the top of his head. "Tomorrow we'll phone. I don't know what I've been thinking."

He turns and lays his head on my chest. "I'm sorry, honey. I just can't anymore."

We sit there for a long time in the dark. When we finally get to bed, I keep that picture in front of me all night, a picture of the old man weeping on the stairs. I can smell the tang of wet wood, and I can't believe how old we've become. Even when I double my 4:00 a.m. dose to fill the cave in the middle of my body, I keep that picture in front of me.

Dying is one thing–it happens. But getting old so unfits my picture of us that I have to keep his bent, weeping frame in front of me so I can get things organized. Get my pictures to fit with where we are.

The sun doesn't clear the trees until about eleven now. But when it does, it warms everything right up. I take my coffee out to the porch and put my feet up on the bench, watching for him to bring the mail. The trees have lost their leaves. The last time I went to town they were still green but for a few poplars on the south-facing slopes.

The pickup pulls around the bend, and for a minute I think I see two heads. I blink to clear my vision, to smile, but he stops down by the pasture. I hear metal clanging, a cow bellowing and a couple of slaps.

Then he drives right up to the house and I almost cry out when I see a woman's shape climb out from where I should be sitting. I can imagine him loading the truck with the few things around here he cares about and leaving. Fed up. Then I remember. The homemaker.

"Honey," he says, "you don't have to wait until the home service gets its act together. Help is at hand."

He's all phony bright and cheerful as he brings Nadia up the stairs. I can see he's completely tickled.

He leans in close and I smell coffee on his breath, coffee and something else, something so faint it's hardly a smell. He leans in closer and says in my hair, "Just play along, girl. Look at the child's fingers. You've got your work cut out for you."

I watch her face carefully as she looks me over. It's been almost a year since I've seen her, and I watch for the cloud when she gets a good look. Nothing.

"I was asking a friend if I could borrow her truck to pick up one of my cows–" she begins.

He butts in. "I was sitting at the counter and overheard. Said my truck was right there and available."

It all tumbles out, both of them interrupting, laughing, excited.

She doesn't have much good fence, but was going to tether the cow, hope the calf stuck around, couldn't stand not having any, didn't figure her husband would even notice for a few days, if ever.

"It'll be months before there's a settlement," she says. "I'll pop over in the morning, feed the cows, do a little tidying here. Your husband says I'll be able to see them from the kitchen window when I do the dishes."

She is watching me carefully to see how I'm taking this. He's not watching, carefully too.

Her chewed fingers, reddened and chapped, take one of my hands gently.

"We'll see," I say. And I see his shoulders, bending into the refrigerator for some cream, relax, and he comes up smiling.

Delivery

"Jimmy, you deliver this one," Watson had told me.

He'd laughed and Florrie had laughed with him. I'd felt as left out as the boy minding the door at a poker game. Just like that. A kid again. For a minute, yakking with Florrie McKinnon on the steps of the train station, I'd felt older. She was sitting in the sun, bouncing a baby on her lap.

She'd gone to school with my older brother and she'd always been a looker. Red hair, white skin, and long legs. Hadn't seen her in a while and suddenly here she was, sitting in the spring sunshine. She wore a flowered dress, belted at the waist, and a white cardigan, kind of lacy. Girls back then always had a white cardigan they'd bring out around Easter.

The kid was bouncing and laughing. I didn't think anything of it. In those days with big families and hardly any cars, we were always hauling kids around. Could be one of your own family's, a neighbour's, anybody's.

"Where've you been?" I asked.

"Back east, living with my aunt. Old witch. I was getting sick of housework and early nights."

She stuck her face in the baby's neck and blew.

"I decided to hightail it home."

She looked around the grimy station, at Watson watching her. "Now I'm not sure it was such a great idea." She lifted her face to the sun.

Her skin was so pale the veins on her throat looked like lines of blue ink. She was warm, you could tell; her hair curled damply at the back of her neck. I was just taking this all in, about to ask her how long she'd been in town, when Watson called me. And smiled his smirky smile.

I delivered telegrams after school. He'd have them ready for me. At first I didn't know what was in them. He wouldn't give me the bad ones though–the ones about jail, death, or bankruptcy. He liked to personally deliver anything that might give him leverage. Whenever anyone saw me coming that spring, they knew it was nothing serious. Oh, it's just Jimmy, they'd think.

So when I climbed on my bike that breathless afternoon, the cottonwood smell swelling the air to thick and heavy syrup, I wasn't prepared. Mr. Thomas McGill, 3234 Phillips Avenue. Didn't seem like any big deal. All I was thinking about was that girl and the look of the sun on her throat. Her teasing me about not getting mixed up, with only one telegram to deliver.

When I think back though, Watson was edgy, like he was uncomfortable about this one. He called out after me, "Mind you give it right to him–not the old woman. Into his hands. And wait for an answer."

He knew what was in all the telegrams, of course, and he had a soft way of making sure, without saying a word, that people knew he did. When you came to meet someone at the train, he'd let on he knew who was coming and why. He'd discuss stock prices with the bank manager, Mr. Leland, prices he'd read off the teletype. And he'd take the elbows of the bereaved, solicitous before they knew they'd lost someone. He was unpleasant somehow–underhanded. But careful. What he talked about, he could have picked up in the coffee shop.

After I took over, that changed. I never spoke once to anyone about any of the telegrams. Not even Mary Ellen. She would look at me with her eyebrows raised and I'd shake my head. Poor Mary Ellen, she'd be the last to know.

Now that I think of it, I hadn't even met Mary Ellen that spring. I was only fifteen and knew nothing about anything that mattered. But I do remember that afternoon. When I wheeled away from the station, my blood ran as slow and thick as the cottonwood air. As I rode through the sleepy streets, I felt like all the fun in the world was happening somewhere else, like I'd entered a room recently vacated. All the signs of activity were there: neatly mown lawns still unraked, freshly clipped shrubs, a heap of pink cherry blossoms, newly tilled vegetable patches, rows marked with hopeful string. But not a child in sight, not a mother bringing in the laundry hanging limp in the unmoving air, no one clearing the abandoned pop bottles off the picnic tables.

Some sprinklers swished, oblivious to the black clouds bruising the eastern sky and stilling every breeze as they spread across the valley. I remember thinking that Florrie would soon be buttoning that cardigan right up to her chin and scurrying home, that it was a good thing her family lived near the station.

I rode along, trying to keep my shoulder bag from bumping against my knee and listening to the clank of the chain hitting the dent in the rusty chain guard. I tried to place Mr. McGill. In those days this town was pretty small and people mostly stayed put. You didn't know everyone, but you knew who everyone was.

It was odd something didn't immediately come to mind, because I remembered later I'd overheard my brother and his buddies talking about him. But my mother had always shut her mouth tight and looked blank whenever anyone tried to give her a bit of juicy news, so we never heard many details of other folks' lives at our dinner table. We didn't have the habit of piecing gossip together.

Thinking of it now, it's pretty funny–later on, I came to know more dirt and misery about the people in this town than even old

Dr. Maynard. It was like my mother had been training me for the job. And Mary Ellen, she just gave up asking. What my eyes read on those thin telegraph tapes went into my brain, all right, but couldn't find a way out.

When my brother was killed at the roadhouse near Treacher, I got the telegram. I was learning the news while I was piecing the tape together. It was the oddest feeling, like the hand holding the paper cutter didn't belong to me, like I was watching someone else paste down that message. I even remember I had a hangnail on my index finger and thought how it looked like it should be sore. But I couldn't feel it, not on my own hand.

Even worse, I had to tell my mother. By then I knew better than to try to ease the news. She leaned against the door frame, her face expressionless as her eyes moved across the telegram. She just shook her head and looked out at the street like her older son's death was what she'd expected.

"Jimmy, it's dirty work you've got" was all she said, and then walked away and called Dad. I stood there, my head leaning lightly against the screen of the door until Dad noticed me. I can still remember the feel of that screen against my forehead.

In any case, as was usual that spring, I had a distinct shortage of information. By the time the first clumsy raindrops puffed in the red dust of the road, all I'd remembered about Mr. McGill were some whispers. He'd been a teacher at the high school a few years before, when my brother was still getting into scraps there. McGill had come out from Ontario with a pretty young wife and his mother, but the wife had disappeared. Left him, I guess. Then, for some reason unfit for my ears to hear, he'd had to leave the school. I soon enough found out why, but there on my bike I couldn't even think what he looked like.

I was still idly stringing along thoughts of Florrie and my brother and McGill when the rain started in earnest. Phillips Avenue was at the south end of town, past the school and down the trail through the old burnt-out hospital property across the tracks. You could reach it by road, but that meant going way round to get to the level crossing. It's where that new hotel is now, where all the government types stay.

Anyway, by the time I got through the trail, I wasn't thinking about the telegram anymore. Or Florrie. I was worried about the trip back through those twisting shallow-rooted spruces. There's always a few fall over, splintering and cracking in the gusts that come with the spring storms we get around here. And the great dead branches that come spiralling, crashing off the tops of the old cottonwoods.

So when I jumped off my bicycle in front of the gate with 3234 Phillips neatly painted on the gatepost, I was about as curious as a drowned cat–all I wanted was to get out of striking distance of the lightning.

But for some reason I stood there for a second, careful to balance the bike against the post. Water drops beaded on its paint, running down and dripping onto the lilies blooming below. I'd ridden by this gate hundreds of times on my way to the eddy in the river where we swim all August, but I'd never thought about what lay behind it.

So the garden was my first surprise. When I lifted the latch and swung the gate open, it stopped me right there. Everything was bursting and swelling–lilacs, forsythia, hyacinths, flowering crab, daffodils, and tiny little blue flowers as thick in the grass as dandelions.

The lightning seemed to have pressed all the oxygen out of the air–I could barely catch my breath as I hurried down the narrow path toward the house. The water was everywhere, pouring from the sky, dripping from the flowers and shrubs crowding the flagstones, already pooling in the grass. My hair was streaming and I licked the water collecting in a drop at the tip of my nose.

The house had one of those tiny glassed-in porches you still see in the older parts of town. They're silly things, cold and damp most times of the year, but appealing just the same. This one was full of potted plants–geraniums, petunias. I was never much of a gardener, but I remember the names. The feed store would order seeds and bulbs through us, and getting those lists of names straight was a bugger. There is a big difference between a peony and a petunia, I found out.

I shook the water out of my hair and stepped inside to knock on the inner door. Mrs. McGill, the mother, was my next surprise. This was in the days when women of a certain age never, and I mean never, wore slacks, when they put on a girdle and stockings every morning and wore dresses that rustled against the stiff nylon undergarments. I'd heard this woman's rustle before because I'd see her every few weeks down at the office. She had some arrangement with Watson, I knew, because he always looked like he was expecting her. He'd bring her in behind the wicket to sit down while they conducted their business. Once I saw money change hands, so she must have been buying a money order.

She scared me somehow. And not only me. There were always a few loafers hanging around the station, and whenever she walked in things quieted right down. People didn't go about their business. They just waited for her to leave.

She intrigued me too. You could see she didn't like dealing with Watson, and she didn't care if he noticed. I admired her for that. Not caring what he thought of her. Where my mother was cold, she was hot, if that makes any sense. Fierce.

So, when she opened the door, I stammered. Stammering got me through a lot of potentially complicated conversations. Like whether I was supposed to indicate that we'd met before.

She'd take the telegram for Mr. McGill, she said.

I stammered some more. Stuff about person-to-person and how if he wasn't here I could come back later.

She looked at me closely, and I could feel her heat. There was a musty smell of cabbages and pot roast coming from the rooms behind her, and in the middle of it I could smell her. A sour smell. Women are damp and heat all at once, all thrown together. They smoulder like green wood. Even my mother's coolness could burn you like freezing metal on your tongue. Girls seem different, but they aren't. I thought again of Florrie's damp hair.

"I don't want him disturbed," she said. "He's gardening."

I looked at her, then out at the rain. We could hardly hear each other, it was coming down so hard. I sneezed. I was cold now, and irritable. Spring in this part of the world can be warm enough, but the heat doesn't hold. The cold air swirls down out of the mountains and can freeze things up even in June. I wanted to get moving.

"I didn't see anyone," I said.

"He's probably taken cover in the back shed." I could tell she didn't like having to explain. I waited for directions. "But he won't like an interruption."

What a waste of bloody time, I thought, and turned to go. I heard her call, "You're sure I can't sign for it?" but I stomped down the steps. Watson would love this. One telegram to deliver and I couldn't manage it. I was thinking this when I decided to follow the path around the back, though I didn't think there'd be anyone there. So McGill was surprise number three.

I heard him first. Faintly. He'd called out to me. Then I saw him. He sat on a covered lawn swing. The rain was a roaring curtain between us. I paused at the edge of the sodden grass watching him drift back and forth. The thunder crackled and thudded behind him. I knew he was her son when I saw his eyes, the same stony colour. As I crouched under the swing's awning, I realized he'd been drinking. He lounged across from me like this was some garden party. The rain enclosed us, the air thick with the smell of lilacs and whiskey.

"Mr. McGill?" It sounded like I was accusing him. He wasn't very old, I realized. Late twenties.

He smiled, a sly smile on a pale mouth, and nodded.

"Gardening?" I persisted, feeling nasty.

He blushed. I was tickled to see the red creep up and out to the tips of his ears.

"I have this telegram, personal for Mr. Thomas McGill. So I have to make sure I deliver it to the right person, see," I continued. I'd heard my brother talk like this enough times to have my tone right.

"There's no need to be offensive, young man," he said suddenly, and I could hear the schoolteacher in him. I didn't care. I imagined Florrie listening, approving.

"Well, do you want your telegram or not?"

He put out his hand. It was large and dirty.

I hauled out my book for him to sign. He scrawled and then sat back. He looked out through the rain and took a deep breath. He didn't plan to open it while I was there. I could see that. People have different ways of receiving a telegram. Some wipe hands clean on anything handy and carefully peel back the flap. Others rip them in half, unfold the bits, and piece them back together, like they can fix whatever's inside. Some even ask me to read it for them. But everyone itches to know what's inside. I found myself very curious.

"I was told to wait for an answer."

He looked toward the house. "An answer," he said slowly, staring past me. I turned and saw his mother watching from a window, her face blurred behind the water-streaked glass.

"Someone out there is waiting right now to hear back, Mr. McGill," I said, enjoying myself. I don't know where I got my nerve, talking to him like that. It wasn't like me. But, for a few minutes I felt, at last, in control of something.

McGill waved to his mother. You could almost feel the pull between them. If it hadn't been pouring like that, he'd have gone inside to read it, and who knows what would have happened. But he stayed and opened the flap. His lips moved as he spelled out the message.

The first thing he did was look back toward the house and wave again. Then he turned slightly so she couldn't see his face, and the sly look crept back across it. He folded the telegram carefully and patted his pockets as if looking for something. It was weird. All my big ideas went *poof.* The way he was acting, I felt like I'd vanished. He looked at his watch, stepped out of the swing, and wiped his hands on the grass. The rain was letting up. He put his hand on my elbow and walked me toward the gate.

His mother called from the porch. "Tom, your supper's ready." He stiffened for a minute, then touched his shoulder, as if to brush away a hand.

"I'm just seeing this young gentleman to the gate, Mother.

Teaching him a little horticulture. I'll be right in."

She stared, then slammed the door. She knew there was trouble, but she miscalculated its proximity. She figured it could wait for the pot roast.

As soon as we stepped outside the gate, McGill started tearing lilacs off the bush and talking fast.

"Listen, son," he said, "could you lend me your bike, just for a few minutes?" He had bunched the flowers into a bouquet and was twisting the telegram around the stems to hold them together.

I said nothing. Something big had happened and I was back minding the door and not getting any of the jokes whirling in the smoky room filled with drinking men.

"I'll pay you," he said. "There's a good lad. Here's five bucks."

I was deflated, as flat as an old bike tire. "Go ahead," I said, extracting the bill from his damp fingers. As I watched him rattle up the road, the low evening sun shone through the scattered rain that still fell. My head felt as slow as if it had just received a blow. I was trying to figure out what had happened when I heard Mrs. McGill calling from the porch. I scuttled away myself, too late to yell after her son about where was he going anyway, and where was I going to pick up my bike.

I laugh now when I think about it. What I had witnessed, sure as shooting, was a man springing to attention and following his reverberating prick to the object of its desire. That hot little telegram must have told him she was at the station, waiting. Him sitting there in his swing inhaling damp flowers like some slug, jolted into action. As long as she was out of town and he felt the burning weight of his mother's hand on his shoulder, he'd sit still. But put the girl that close and he was able to spring loose as long as he sprung fast. I know that feeling well, myself, with a mother like mine.

Watson, the bastard, chortled when I showed up an hour later.

"They caught the eastbound train," he said. "I've never seen a getaway like it."

When I saw my bike leaning against the counter, I didn't have to ask who.

"She sat here half the day, knowing just the right amount of time to give him, to get out of here before his mother knew what was happening. She checked with me about how long it would take to be delivered. She had their tickets and everything all ready. A clever little cookie, that one." He laughed. "Though why she's wasting her time on him, I'll never know. Not when there's others available." He puffed out his chest. "Did he ever look the fool, racing in here with those ratty flowers. Like a big wet puppy slavering after a bone."

"What did the telegram say?"

He looked at me sideways. "You know better than to ask the contents of a telegram," he said, then laughed again. "Though it was beautifully composed, if I do say so myself."

I knew then he'd helped her write it. Probably leaned close enough to breathe in her warmth. My skin crawled. I looked at the empty platform, saw the lilacs scattered, trodden.

When their telegram came a week later, from Vancouver, Watson asked me to deliver it. I looked at him. Florrie's family had already told everyone in town.

"Why don't you leave it until she comes in like usual?"

"Oh, I doubt if she'll be sending any more money Florrie's way," Watson said. "That whole scheme backfired right in her face. She underestimated Miss Florrie McKinnon. That girl was not cut out for housework and threats of everlasting damnation."

I agreed to deliver the telegram. I was curious about the old woman. There was no chill in the air now and the rains of the week before had hatched the mosquitoes, that first, nasty brood. I was sweating and swatting when I opened the gate again. I could still see where the lilacs had been torn away.

Inside it was pitiful. The lawn was mowed close, all the little blue flowers shorn. The shrubs had been pruned back to sticks, the flower beds clipped. It was like seeing a woman with her head shaved. Brutal.

You know you hear those stories about people sitting peacefully in their chairs and just burning up, leaving nothing behind but their slippers? Well, so much wrath boiled out of Mrs. McGill when she looked at that telegram, I thought she might ignite. I felt singed. I was jealous then, of all three of them. Like a magnifying glass had collected stray light and focused it into one scorching point. Illuminating them.

When I got back, Watson asked me how she'd taken to the wedding announcement. "That Florrie." He smirked. "She signed it Mrs. Thomas McGill."

I pretended not to know what he was talking about. When school was over that year, I was ready to run my own errands. Thought I'd try my hand working in the bush. If you'd asked me then, I'd have said I'd never be back.

Breathing Fire

June 21. National Aboriginal Day. And there's Eddie up on the bandstand welcoming the Indians to town. Laughing when they bring out the big scissors to cut the ribbon across the doorway to their new office. Nodding to the drums, watching the kids dance.

Maybe things have changed, after all.

After all what? After he kicked old Minnie Jack out of his store for loitering, not knowing she had bad arthritis, needed to sit a while, and was a big chief besides. After he and his buddies bought up those lots down by the river where the Indians used to live and got the fire chief to burn down their cabins for fire practice. After he crawled out of Frankie's Roadhouse. After all. My mother's voice bitter in my ears.

Eddie didn't look so much the sober citizen the night the roadhouse went up in smoke. Fact is, none of us came out of there looking much good. And one of us ended up dead. One life weighed against the demise of Frankie's Roadhouse. Some said it was worth it.

If things had been different, I might have been one of them.

Frankie's Roadhouse. Out near Treacher. A good car ride away from town where the Chinese restaurant closed at eight. Where the beer parlour closed at midnight. The drive home long enough to talk a girl into something foolish. Long enough to sober you up, so's you could sneak in past your mother.

Didn't burn down soon enough for me.

⁂

The air short in your lungs, Jimmy. Old wood full of road dust and dirt flaking off men who never washed themselves or their clothes, flaking off as they bent their elbows to drink. All catching fire and leaving the air short of what your lungs hunger for.

⁂

He had one of those mixed-up names they saddled the Indians with. Tommy George. George Tommy. Georgie Tom. Little boys' names. He said to call him Thomas.

⁂

They say I wasn't there when my ma's house burnt. I remember it though. Same feeling. The fire sucked into your chest. Old planks suddenly dancing. Flashing and sparking. There was never enough air.

⁂

I was tired of being a kid. Being little Jimmy delivering telegrams after school, women messing my hair like I was still ten. Eddie's dad slipping me a quarter to drop a bet with my boss who ran a nice little sports pool out of the telegraph office. Right from this building here, beside what used to be the train station. When you think of the Indians setting up here in the old federal building, it makes you laugh. Former home to the Mounties, the jail. Indians'd get thrown in there for spitting on Main Street.

The phone company was in there too. The operators sat up on high stools routing phone calls, sparking my afternoons with swinging ankles, with the nyloned knees some would let slide out from under their skirts when they saw me looking. They knew my good Catholic mother would freeze me into a pillar of salt if she suspected I even thought about those knees. And make me quit my job.

I was tired of window-shopping.

⁂

You didn't like Frankie's, did you, Jimmy? Didn't like the smell of it. I could tell, easy, as soon as we walked in that door. It was the only place would serve Indians. Hotel restaurants wouldn't let us in the door.

⁂

The first time I went in there, we were fresh off the train from Halifax. English so thick on my dad's Dutch tongue that Frankie, a stocky little guy had blond hair then, had a hard time understanding what he wanted. Looking for the man who sponsored us to immigrate. Farmer down by the river. Me standing behind my big brother in the doorway, letting in the flies. Cigarette smoke and fried food. Coffee a little burnt. Bright red tables and counter. Twirling soda fountain stools like we'd seen in American movies.

⁂

Uncle liked to take me there when we came out of the bush. Teach me how to handle the white guys, he'd say. When to joke along with them. When to keep my mouth shut.

⁂

I was barely sixteen the winter I went sawmilling. Thomas the same age. Four years before the fire at Frankie's. Us Dutchies were at the bottom of the pecking order in those places, down with the Indians.

Thomas knew how to survive in a winter bush camp. How to cull warmth from the horses. How to keep out of the way of trees falling into four feet of snow. Keep hands out of the saw blade. It was thanks to him I came out of the bush with all my fingers and the understanding that I was not cut out for that life. Went back to the telegraph, back to operator's knees and lovesick Mounties.

⁂

You're right not to stray too far from that clean office. You're not cut out for fights, people throwing up in corners, grannies crying as their families die all around them.

⁂

I looked like any other Canadian backwoods boy in those days. Made people forget we'd lived through the Nazi occupation. Had seen death every day: street executions, bodies in our kitchen, their skin like wax. And worse. Snitches. Collaborators. It had burned my mother into something hard and fierce. She hated it here. How can people let their guard down like that? she'd ask whenever things got a little rowdy in town. She raised her kids when even laughing out loud in public was dangerous, much less shouting drunken abuse in the street. When you're drunk, you'll say anything. You'll get people killed, she would hiss.

The Dutch came full of admiration for Canadians. Could never figure out why they treated us so bad. But not my mother. Her fury grew with every overheard insult. They're no different than the Germans, she'd say.

⋙

My uncle hauling me out on the trapline as soon as the ground froze, to get me out of harm's way. But worrying every winter some big white asshole gonna be there with his rifle and his face burned rough and red from the cold. Slam the door of our own cabin in our faces. Or find all that's left is a pile of burned timbers.

⋙

Thomas's mother was Sophie. The pall of her burning still hung over town when we arrived. A few of us white kids and all those silent Indians going to the Catholic school. Walking past the ashes and the muttering. Another Indian drinking. Wood stoves. Incineration. The Canadian crematorium, my mother said. That was a word we knew. Same in Dutch as in English.

⋙

Before Ma died, we'd spend winters in town. I'd pull the toboggan, and Ma and me'd pick scraps of wood from the lumber yard out back of the store. Eddie's pa, he owned the place. Sometimes he'd stick his head out the door and he and my ma'd talk. Joke back and forth. Sometimes that Eddie was there and we'd play around a bit. Hide-and-seek in the lumber. I liked going there. Eddie'd give me candy if he had any.

⋙

My mother, she never forgave my father for losing his courage. For bringing us here. She had turned him into some kind of hero during the war. In the resistance, delivering messages, hiding people. But later, when the planes started flying over during the Berlin blockade, every night the planes going over just like in the war, my dad cracked like one of those old paintings, the varnish shattering into a million crazy lines. He finally wrote his brother who was already here–to get us out.

⁂

Eddie's dad, he'd come over with a bottle of rye. Ma would put me to bed in the back room and give me a bucket to piss in. I had to stay in the room. It'd be cold back there and sometimes when things quieted down I'd crack the door to let the heat in. That old burner. You could see the fire flickering red through the draft, a red cross of flame.

⁂

Eddie was the only son of one of the old boys. Born too late to be in on the newness of things here. The firstness. The first hotel, the first car, the first white baby. Had to listen to the stories with nothing of his own to throw in.

⁂

Eddie's ma. Almost makes me feel sorry for what I did to him. She saw us out back of the store one day. Must have known about me. Dragged him away screaming out things at my ma like I'd never heard before. Edward, she called him. Her lips drawn back, hard and white.

⁂

Poor Eddie. I remember his mother at the high school, organizing elocution contests, ballroom dancing classes. Her lipstick slipping sideways. Used the bottom of a gin bottle for a mirror, my brother said.

⁂

I got to thinking our fire was Eddie's bitch of a mother's eye watching me. I didn't want to go back, but Ma laughed at her raving and dragged me down there a couple of days later to get more wood. It was about then I'd wake up screaming, burning up. My aunties would hush me. They told me I was come back from Johnny King. He went in that big fire at Fishkill Lake. I had the mark of his burns on my back, they said. I was a warning to Ma.

Frankie's was where my brother died. My sweet-talking lady's man brother who defied our mother from the day he set foot in Canada. Never guarded his mouth or his wandering hands. Got knifed in the parking lot buying rye from his girlfriend's old sweetheart. Frankie sent him out there, then locked the door. Wouldn't answer my brother's yelling. Thought he was just drunk and rowdy, he told the cops. Stayed behind the locked door while my brother bled his brightness into the sweet summer solstice–1956.

Brothers. I'm nothing like he was. That little dough boy I let the air out of. He needed sticking.

Everyone is always dying. My mother's words at three in the morning after we buried my brother. When will they stop dying?

I didn't know he was my dad. It's different with my people. Your mother gives you your clan. Your uncles take you out onto the territory. No one talked about it.

I remember the smell of ashes in the cold Monday morning on the way to school. Just after we got here. Sophie's ashes.

⸙

She'd yell when he brought his friends. Limp bills. Limp and sticky from fat, white fingers, fat, white maggots. Turning and lifting everything on the table. Salt shaker, sugar spoon, ashtray. Eddie's got them same fingers. I saw them last night at Frankie's. Handling everything on the table. His thumb moving across the holes on the salt shaker. I'm glad he's dead. I just wish his old man was dead too. Them all telling me I wasn't there that night when every night I dream it. The stove so hot. He must have snuck home to his wife. Dick still sticky. Left the damper open.

⸙

Been a couple of years since I'd seen him, that night Thomas walked into Frankie's with his uncle. June 21. The solstice. Darkness already on its secret return, darkness hidden in long evening light. It was an anniversary I liked to draw to Frankie's attention. Remind him about my brother. I'd sit at the small table by the washrooms and watch him working his charm. I'd never get drawn into his talk.

Thomas nodded to me and steered his uncle around shell-shocked Andy Olsen and Elly shuffling around the floor. Patti Page singing, "How much is that doggy in the window?"

"About fifteen bucks!" someone yelled. "Go get her, Andy."

A booth spilling eight or ten people. It was Saturday night and they were finally feeling relief from the pain of Friday night. Half of them underage, though Frankie didn't have a licence to sell liquor to anybody anyways.

Elly's pouchy face twisted and she shoved Andy off her shoulder, grabbed her purse off the table, and tottered back to the washrooms.

Thomas and his uncle Billy sat on the two stools at the end of the counter. Looking away from me. Away from the table full of trouble.

"What'll it be, boys?"

"Uncle?"

"Whatever you got going under the counter there."

"A plate of fries with gravy. Coke."

"See what I can do. The fryer's acting up." Frankie had to walk by me to get into the kitchen. I watched him.

Mavis plugged some nickels into the jukebox.

"Hey, Mavis, how about Bill Haley? Let's get things rocking in here." Eddie. Half her age. Trying to flaunt his little ruffed grouse tail. His mom still making him stick it out at high school. When I look at kids that age now, I can't believe any of us were ever that young.

Frankie brought out the fries. Poured more drinks. A few more people wandered in, too restless to sleep nights when it never really got dark, just dimmed into evening about midnight. Ribbing each other. Jokes about the songs. About women. White bread and toast. Indian women were toast. Sometimes they forgot to take them out of the toaster and they burned. That was the kind of talk you'd hear at night in Frankie's. Indian women sitting right there.

Thomas's uncle got to talking about Sophie. About what a wonderful mother she was to Thomas. How smart she was. The nuns wanted to keep her in school longer but for that bastard knocking her up. Thomas squirming, his fries eaten, his glass empty. His uncle getting louder.

"Let's go, Uncle."

This happened all the time in small towns. Trying to stop things that half the town already knew from getting said out loud. Talking over the heads of the kids, of newcomers. You knew information was moving around, but you didn't know what it was really about, who it was really aimed at.

Frankie said to Eddie, "Your old man liked his toast well-done."

Eddie was pretty well pickled by that time. Leaning on Mavis. Fiddling with the mess of dirty dishes, knives, the ketchup bottle on the table. Thomas was hauling on his uncle.

Frankie was usually pretty good at making things lively, but still keeping the lid on. I wonder if it was me sitting there watching his moves–his hands on people's shoulders, his teasing–goaded him to go a little further. He knew my mother, knew me. Knew I didn't like that kind of talk any better'n Thomas did.

Because he broke the rules and said it out loud. When one of Eddie's friends said if you scraped off the outer layer, gave her a good scrubbing, why almost any squaw was a tasty little piece, Frankie broke through the laughter.

"But you've got to be careful because you never know what you might catch," he said. "Something musta got into your dad's business because he had the juice to pop out one." He pointed at Eddie. "And two." He pointed at Thomas. "Just like that, and then that's it. No more."

The silence lasted about a second. Then a big whoop exploded and one wiseass said, "Better watch out, Eddie, or he'll be after a share in the business."

I was on my feet, already wishing I had never heard any of this. Never wanting to hear secrets laid open. Uncle Billy fell off his stool on his way to get Frankie. Thomas wrestled the steak knife out of his hand and stalled there in the middle of the floor like a pit-lamped deer.

Eddie said, "Don't you go trying to pin that little shit on my old man. From what I hear half of Main Street could have done the job."

Thomas was on him before the yelling really began and Eddie was fighting back when the deep fryer caught on fire. It didn't exactly explode, but the flames were suddenly everywhere. Screaming and the flames sucking all the air out of your lungs. Thomas's shirt was smoking when I pulled him off Eddie and dragged him outside. It flamed up in the open air. I was rolling him around on the ground when he stopped me. "Where's Uncle Billy?

I patted down his shirt one more time and got up to have a look. Billy was slumped under the big spruce drooping beside the door. Could have gone up any second. While I dragged him out of the fire's path, Mavis started screaming, "Where's Eddie? Where's Eddie?"

The roadhouse was a bright flame, its exploding windows shooting hot tongues of light. The roar drowned everything.

Five or six men loomed over Thomas, quiet in his pain on the gravel. Mavis was there too. "Murderer," she sobbed. "Murderer." One of the men bent to take the knife out of Thomas's hand. Another's boot nudged him.

"He's burnt pretty bad," I said. "I'll get him to the hospital."

"This boy's not going to any hospital," one man said. "If he goes anywhere at all, he's going to jail."

I don't know what would've happened if I hadn't been there, if I hadn't sat down there on the gravel beside Thomas and waited for the police to get wind of another hot night down at Frankie's Roadhouse. Thinking I'd saved his bacon.

⋙

That little twerp with the fancy truck. Driving rolls of roofing paper and lumber around. If I sometimes wanted a brother, I didn't want one like him. Or a pa like his old man. It makes me sick. His blood flowing through the both of us. I just wanted to let a little bit out.

⋙

Way I see it now, Uncle Billy was right. Frankie was the man to stick. But Frankie knew how to put someone else's hand on the knife before twisting it in.

⋙

How could my uncle's smart sister, my so-called good mother bitch, put out for that bastard's father? How could she do that, Jimmy?

⋙

Sunday, after mass, the priest called my mother in to clean Thomas up from the burns. They'd thrown him in a cell. He thought Eddie had gone up with the roadhouse. She told me to get in there. Make some sense out of what he was saying. I didn't think it would do any good to tell him Eddie'd managed to crawl clear. To tell him Eddie was in a clean white hospital bed.

⋙

It's like I have strings tied to my hands and legs, strings tied to the inside of my head and there's a thousand people twitching on them strings, making me dance like Uncle Johnny in a fit. Or like old Andy last night. Stumbling around the floor. Is Andy dead too, Jimmy?

⋙

He got delirious. I didn't get half of what he said.

⋙

Look at these hands, Jimmy. Look at them squirm like hungry maggots.

⋙

Tried to get the Mounties to call the doctor. Just the creepie crawlies, they said. It'll pass.

⋙

Jimmy, I got my own burns now. Been through the fire at last. Maybe the dreams'll stop.

⋙

Thomas was my friend. Out there in camp he took care of me as easy as his uncle must have done for him out on the trapline. Here, he'd say, change your socks. He made me wash. In the middle of winter's leaching he taught me how to steal warmth wherever I could find it. Why didn't I tell him about Eddie?

Outside the post office Monday morning. That's when I heard what happened. Some guy slapping Eddie's dad on the shoulder. Laughing. Strung himself up in jail, he said. Thought he'd killed your boy. They shook their heads. Least it'll save the taxpayers a trial. And we don't have to worry about Frankie's Roadhouse anymore. That's one mess cleaned up.

It's a terrible country, my mother said. It's supposed to be peacetime, but there's a war going on. The Indians, they just keep dying, she said. Why doesn't it stop?

⋙

Something jolts through me when I watch Eddie up there now. Its power shakes the blood in my shrinking veins. Something older, I'd bet, than love. Deeper than anger. It's not a feeling I'm accustomed to, this somehow electric darkness.

It brings them all close. Thomas. My brother. My mother. Elly and crazy old Andy Olsen. Thomas's Uncle Billy. Eddie's old man. Even Frankie. All gone. Me'n Eddie seem to be the only ones left to remember Frankie's Roadhouse. To remember where the ashes of the old days are scattered.

SHEILA PETERS has worked as a reporter, weaver, human-rights activist, and English instructor. Her nonfiction book, *Canyon Creek: A Script*, was recently published by Creekstone Press. Peters's stories have appeared in numerous literary journals, including *Prism international*, *Grain*, *Room of One's Own*, *The Malahat Review*, and *Event*. She lives in Smithers, British Columbia.